CITY WALLS

Dr. Jekyll and Mr. Holmes
Peeper
Gas City*
Journey of the Dead*
The Rocky Mountain Moving Picture
Association*
Roy & Lillie: A Love Story*
The Confessions of Al Capone*
The Eagle and the Viper*
Paperback Jack*

PAGE MURDOCK SERIES
The High Rocks*
Stamping Ground*
Murdock's Law*
The Stranglers
City of Widows*
White Desert*
Port Hazard*
The Book of Murdock*
Cape Hell*
Wild Justice*

WESTERNS
The Hider
Aces & Eights*
The Wolfer
Mister St. John
This Old Bill
Gun Man

Bloody Season
Sudden Country
Billy Gashade*
The Master Executioner*
Black Powder, White Smoke*
The Undertaker's Wife*
The Adventures of Johnny Vermillion*
The Branch and the Scaffold*
Ragtime Cowboys*
The Long High Noon*
The Ballad of Black Bart*

NONFICTION
The Wister Trace
Writing the Popular Novel

*Published by Tor Publishing Group

CITY WALLS

An Amos Walker Novel

Loren D. Estleman

Tor Publishing Group
New York

CITY WALLS

A Forge Book
Published by Tom Doherty Associates / Tor Publishing Group
120 Broadway
New York, NY 10271

www.tor-forge.com

Forge® is a registered trademark of Macmillan Publishing Group, LLC.

The Library of Congress Cataloging-in-Publication Data is available upon request.

ISBN 978-1-250-82733-3 (hardcover)
ISBN 978-1-250-82734-0 (ebook)

Our books may be purchased in bulk for promotional, educational, or business use. Please contact your local bookseller or the Macmillan Corporate and Premium Sales Department at 1-800-221-7945, extension 5442, or by email at MacmillanSpecialMarkets@macmillan.com.

First Edition: 2023

Printed in the United States of America

0 9 8 7 6 5 4 3 2 1

To Charles L. Estleman (Corky),
the big brother everyone else wishes he had

CITY WALLS

ONE

I sewed up the Dowling case in less than a day, and committed only one misdemeanor. That was the record.

Fred Dowling had chiseled half a million from the credit union where he was treasurer, converted it to paper, and headed toward Central America, but he got only as far as Cleveland; which if you wanted to make a joke of it was punishment in itself. I didn't. You can't get better pizza anywhere.

All the credit union wanted was its money back. That was all. I said sure thing. When you need the work the truth just gets in the way.

I paid a call on his wife in Royal Oak, and got a strike on the first cast. She'd been taking online courses in Spanish and Portuguese, depending on which country the couple wound up in; only when it came time to go, he forgot her along with the AC/DC converter. She found a phone number belonging to a Carmen Castor when she jimmied open a drawer in his desk. It was on the Cleveland exchange, but when she tried calling the number several times, no one picked up. Anyway it was a place to start.

The address was in a duplex in Lakewood, a suburb on the Erie shore. It was a Siamese twin of a building with identical front doors and windows in reverse mirror-image. Carmen's bell didn't answer. The woman who lived next door, whose features all tapered to a point, told me her neighbor's business wasn't any of hers; but I might try Black-and-White Taxi. That was the sign on the cab Carmen had piled into yesterday with about six months' worth of luggage. Seventeen was the number of the cab. It wasn't any of her business, she said again.

Black-and-White operated out of a tin hut on top of an underground garage. Rows of keys hung on the back wall, attached to miniature soccer balls. The red-headed dispatcher poked my twenty into a breast pocket with *Larry* scripted across it, ran a finger down his clipboard, and said the driver I wanted was off duty; another twenty would get me the address to his house. I got it from a hack I found smoking near the garage ramp for five. That took me back east toward Edgewater Park, but the contact there was more generous still, and directed me to the St. Clair Hotel downtown in return for half a pack of cigarettes; he'd run out.

Cleveland's a good town that doesn't know it isn't supposed to be ugly, so it's quaint. But the granite Indians flanking the bridge over the Cuyahoga always make my skin crawl. In addition to being unpretentious and comfortably dowdy, the place is haunted.

The St. Clair was built to accommodate the visitors that would throng to the Rock and Roll Hall of Fame, and for a while they had. Then the novelty had turned dirty yellow along with the synthetic alabaster façade; but the hotel still attracted enough convention interest to keep up appearances, at least in the lobby. Deep braided chairs stood about any old way on machine-made Navajo rugs and the fleshy leaves belonging to the plants had holes chewed in them; you can't fool bugs with plastic. Everything was just a little bit shabby, but still genteel, if only for the time being, like country tweeds broken in by the butler so they won't whistle while the master strolls the grounds.

I screwed my flanks into the hollow in a cushion and waited. I had a view of the concierge's desk. The sun was sinking and the supper crowd had begun to line up there to find out the best places to eat. Embezzlers had expensive tastes; I was counting on that. If Dowling didn't show up there that night, I'd have to try something else.

It was the last week of September. The open air of the lobby was a little chilly; here in what the Coastals call the Heartland, we shut down the air conditioners on Labor Day and don't turn on the heat before Halloween. A little pneumonia is a small price to pay for life on the Great Lakes. Most of those in line had on light topcoats.

The queue petered out just as it got dark outside. I was getting up to go out for a smoke when the elevator doors opened and Dowling came out with a blonde on his arm. She wasn't tall, she had heavy features, and nothing she wore matched. That made her just the sort of woman a man who spent most of his time balancing numbers on his nose would choose to run off with. Round-faced and scowling, with a hairline that started practically at his eyebrows, he had on a knee-length gray coat with a fake fur collar. It looked a little well-insulated and way too bulky for the first frost of autumn, but maybe he was more delicate than he appeared. They crossed to the concierge's desk.

"Mr. and Mrs. Donner," he said to the woman sitting there. "We're in four-twenty-seven."

Just then a party of six came down the stairs, making enough noise to drown out the conversation. They were evenly divided as to sex, and whatever they'd been drinking was so thick it came with its own humidity. I didn't try to get close enough to overhear what was being said at the desk. Instead I took a page from the detective's manual and rode the elevator to the fourth floor.

Four-twenty-seven was designed to open with a magnetic card, but a latch is a latch. I pulled out the spring-steel strip that helped my wallet keep its shape, poked the end between the door and the frame, twisted the knob, and applied pressure until the latch snapped back into its socket.

The room was upholstered in ultra-suede, with a queen bed that had been romped on and then smeared all over with skirts and blouses and control-top pantyhose, the way some women unpack when they're going out for the evening. There were more women's clothes in the closet, a couple of men's suits, luggage, and a small steel safe that opened with a tin key that would go out with the guest when he did. The suitcases gave me nothing and the bureau drawers could wait. The safe locked with a dead bolt, so I went to work with a set of dental picks I carry around for fun. It took ten minutes, and all I got was a flowered jewelry wrap that Carmen Castor filled with junk from a shopping channel.

I tossed the rest of the room, put everything back the way I'd found it, and let myself back out. I wasn't disappointed; I might have been, if a man smart enough to bilk a financial institution with branches in six states was dope enough to leave the swag in a hotel room. Likewise, too many employees had access to the safe in the lobby for comfort. Dowling's car was out, too. That was even easier to break into than a toy safe.

There was only one place left; but I'd known that right along. The rest was just routine.

I had to shake my head. Embezzlers are a slap in the face of honest crime. Their cleverness never extends beyond the act itself.

The concierge was a tiny woman of thirty or so, either Polynesian or part Japanese, in a smart suit with clear polish on her nails. She belonged on a key chain.

"I'm meeting Mr. and Mrs. Donner for dinner," I said. "My secretary misplaced the name of the restaurant. Did they happen to stop by and ask you for directions?"

She looked at the card I'd given her. I didn't remember who Adam Windsor was or how his card had found its way into my collection, but INVESTMENT COUNSELOR has the solid ring of probity.

"Are you a guest at the hotel?"

"I haven't checked in yet. I got here late. A tanker rolled over in Dundee."

She gave back the card. "Curious thing. Mr. Donner asked me to recommend a restaurant. He didn't know what it was until I suggested it."

I thought about the cash I'd brought. It's as much a tool of the trade as a set of lock picks, but so's instinct: She wasn't for sale. I put on an embarrassed grin. "Busted. I've got just till the end of the month to make quota or I'm out. My daughter wants a big wedding."

"And I'll bet your mother needs an operation. Do I need to bother security?"

I said that wouldn't be necessary.

A yellow SUV with ST. CLAIR HOTEL pulled up under the canopy while I was standing in front of the door weighing my options. The driver, middle-aged, in a brown uniform and baseball cap, got out. His face was a topographical map of broken blood vessels and his nose was running.

It was a hunch. Hotels that offer a shuttle service usually direct guests to theaters and restaurants who pay to be on their route. The driver was jumpy enough to need a toot, but alert enough to recognize the couple's description. I had a fresh fifty twined around my forefinger. He slid it off without waiting for me to unwrap it. "Blue Giraffe." He gave me the address.

"What sort of place is it?"

"They make you wear a tie."

That was perfect.

I stopped at two men's stores on the way. The first couldn't help me. The next sold me a thigh-length gray coat with a fake fur collar. It was snug, but fit okay as long as I didn't button it. I wore it to the restaurant.

It was a rambling building of many styles, set smack in the middle of a six-lane boulevard so that the traffic was forced to flow around it in both directions. The parking lot would have served a drive-in movie. It screamed roadhouse, but a valet parking stand and only the sky-blue silhouette of a giraffe on the canopy to identify it said the gentry had come along since Prohibition to rescue it from bad company.

I left the car where the rest of the skinflints parked to avoid tipping and thanked a character in a safari outfit for sparing me the ordeal of opening the front door. Inside was a buzz of pleasant conversation, a tasteful mural of animals that don't usually get along gathered around a watering hole, and a podium for the hostess, an aristocratic six-one in a red sheath with a diamond clip on one shoulder strap. She wore some kind of glitter that drew attention to her collarbone; I wondered how she knew that was my weakness. I told her I didn't have a reservation.

"We should have something in twenty minutes," she said. "You can wait at the bar." She tilted her highlighted head toward the coat check station.

"Thanks, I'll keep it with me."

"It's required, I'm afraid. The fire code."

I smiled and said thanks. Some days just keep getting better and better.

The coat check station was a square opening in a wall you had to walk around to get to the dining room. The clerk had on a bush jacket just like the doorman, without the leopard-band hat. It all seemed a long way to go to make a connection.

He stopped playing with his phone as I approached, a pallid type dressed for big game with not much hair on his head. He gave me a square of cardboard with a letter and a number on it and turned to slip my coat onto a hanger. An identical coat hung near it. While his back was to me I leaned in and spotted an open twenty-ounce bottle of Mountain Dew on the shelf below the sill: another break.

I left him and took a seat on a bench by the front door. From there I could see the clerk when I turned my head. When you apply for an investigator's license, sitting is part of the road test.

He went on monkeying with his phone, using just one thumb every time he helped himself to Dew. He had a bladder made of crocodile hide; but I was more patient. Against the smells from the kitchen, the drive-in at Wendy's was a distant memory.

Finally he came out the narrow door next to the opening and turned down the hall to the restrooms without ever looking up from his gizmo. I stood, stretched, and strolled over to his station.

The door was unlocked. I stepped past where my coat was hanging and took its twin off its hanger. It was nearly twice as heavy as mine, but just to make sure I gave the nylon lining a slap. It might have been stuffed with supermarket coupons, but I doubted it. I shrugged into the coat, holding onto the scrap of cardboard as I stepped outside. If the clerk came back and caught me I could always claim I was in a hurry and mistook the coat for mine. A twenty folded around the check wouldn't hurt.

The coast was clear, thanks to kidneys and caffeine.

I kept the coat on as I drove, sweating a little from the extra insulation. I didn't take it off until I checked into a Holiday Inn Express near the ramp to I-80 and locked the door behind me. I used my pocket knife to pop a few threads, enough to pull out a pack of American Express traveler's checks and riffle through them. There must have been several dozen packs like it, with stitches all the way around to keep each from shifting; an inexpert job, but thorough. I returned the pack to its niche and ordered pizza. The deliveryman frowned at my fifty.

"Got anything smaller?'

I grinned. "Sorry."

Afterward I bunched up the coat to make a pillow while I slept.

That was as far as it would get from my hands until I turned it over to the client.

I was a rich man for a night; but I should have driven straight home. Good-luck days never come back-to-back. The next is always as bad as they get.

TWO

The credit union had a branch office on Broadway, in a gunmetal brick building with black-tinted windows that wrapped around it like sunglasses. I put in there, not wanting to carry a dollar that didn't belong to me across the city, much less the state line. Everything about the place duplicated the setup in Detroit, except the receptionist. This one was a young man with moussed hair that lay in flat rows like porcupine quills, who didn't know anything about me or why I was there.

That was no surprise. If the brass didn't want to prosecute Dowling, they didn't want the news that the firm had been fleeced to get beyond the front office. So I sat in a spring-steel chair admiring three walls, one aqua, one salmon, and one Granny Smith while the phone-calling took place, half a million dollars in my lap.

Like most people who haven't any, I respect money. Schlepping the treasure in the lining of a cheap overcoat seemed shabby, so I'd off-loaded it into an Indians gym bag I bought in the hotel gift shop. It was made of vinyl and canvas and smelled like a beach toy.

When the porcupine gave me the high sign I carried it into a private office, where I wandered the room admiring framed monochrome photographs of skyscrapers that no longer existed while a team of executives and accountants counted and recorded the amounts on the travelers' checks. I had to ask the branch manager for my gym bag back after he gave me a receipt.

Maybe it was the name on the bag, or maybe it was too nice a day in late summer to fight my way through the eternal construction on the interstate; but instead of going home I drove to Jacob's Field, where the Indians were hosting the Tigers for first place in the central division. It was one of Cleveland's last games under its century-old name; after that, Custer's job would be finished.

I sat in the nosebleed section of the bleachers, drinking watered-down beer and watching Detroit blow a three-run lead in the sixth. Then Cabrera, trying hard for that milestone home run, smashed one into my section that struck one of the wooden seats six feet behind my head with a noise like a mortar blast; it bounced twice and a fan in a Pistons jersey made a dive for it, body-surfing down the concrete steps in the aisle—woofing on each impact—to come up at last with the ball and enough cracked ribs for a neighborhood barbecue. A couple of his companions supported him between them on their way to Urgent Care. He was green-gilled and had lost most of the skin on one side of his face, but he had enough fight left to keep his friends from prying the ball out of his fist.

He got an ovation from that section. It would have been more lively if the ball had been in fair territory.

Cabrera struck out swinging and the side was retired. I finished my beer during the seventh-inning stretch. Cleveland was ahead by four and my watch gave me just an hour before the homebound traffic caught me in a vise. While I stood arching my back, a light-heavyweight picked his way up the steps in a black suit, white shirt, and black knitted tie, white socks on his ankles. An outfit that far out of place in that venue said he was there for me.

When he got to my tier he turned sideways, shouldering his way past the exodus to the bathrooms and concessions and stopped in front of me, sweating into his collar.

"Kind of formal for a hot-dog vendor," I said, holding out my empty cup. "One for the road."

He took that in better humor than it was intended; that funeral gear during "Take Me out to the Ball Game" annoyed me as much as the play in the outfield.

"I'm not with the park," he said. "Mr. Yale would like to invite you to his suite."

"Where is it?"

He rolled a head the size of a soccer ball in the direction of VIP country. I didn't ask him who Mr. Yale was at all. If he was watching the game from up there, he wouldn't waste time putting me straight.

I followed Black Suit down the steps to the next landing, halfway across the stadium, and up half a mile to the glassed-in section. He led with his left shoulder, the way he would in the ring. On weekends he'd wear a T-shirt that read KISS ME I'M A BODYGUARD.

Once inside the airlock, the conditioned climate drew fog off the broad back of his neck. Mine too, I supposed; but the aroma of shrimp cocktails, steak fajitas, and barrel-aged whiskey kept me from noticing. Windows all around gave a view of the field and all of Cleveland as far as the bridge. Caterers stood around waiting for someone to crook a finger. It was either the team owner's private suite or Hollywood's idea of the Roman baths.

"Mr. Walker?"

A man built along similar lines to the bodyguard, but gone a bit to flab around the middle, crossed an acre of thick carpet in three strides, his hand out. He brushed his iron-gray hair back from a straight line across his forehead, and whatever damage sixty-odd years of living had done to the aquiline features hadn't made them any less arresting in a crowd. It would've looked at home attached to the bare shoulders of a marble bust. He wore a silk sports shirt with the tail untucked, pleated khaki slacks, and Italian loafers, well past broken-in but highly shined. His grip was firm and dry, with scribbler's calluses on his thumb and first three fingers; mechanical pencils stood sentry in his shirt pocket. A University of Detroit class ring had grown into his pinky with most of the embossing worn off.

"Emmett Yale. It *is* Amos Walker, isn't it?"

I admitted it was. "I know who you are, Mr. Yale."

There was no mistaking him in person. *Hour Detroit* said he'd worked his way up from a drafting table in Research and Development at General Motors to a place on the board, then quit to start his own company and design one of the first smart cars to appear since Detroit rediscovered electricity, and had turned down a billion dollars' worth of outside investment in order to remain private and independent. At the moment his company was under federal observation—but not quite investigation—over some crashes involving his signature driverless vehicle on the Yale Mobility proving grounds in Saline.

"You've met Gabe Parrish, my security director?"

"Not formally. Shouldn't he be back at the office, making sure the help doesn't walk out with rubber bands and laser printers?"

"Industrial espionage is his specialty. He's here as my guest."

The prizefighter demonstrated that by pouring himself a drink at the bar. It was club soda. I made a note of that, God knew why.

Yale showed the varnished enamel veneers on his teeth. "I told Gabe that was you up on the Jumbotron, but he likes to argue. You let a souvenir ball fly past your ear."

"My reflexes aren't what they were." I could see the parking-lot-size screen from where we stood; a gaggle of future senators and captains of industry were trying to moon the camera, but none of them could manage his belt buckle and a Big Gulp of Miller Lite at the same time.

I turned a little more attention to Gabe then. When the help acquires a name, I stash it in my wallet for closer examination later. The bodyguard—that was the part he looked, I was wedded to it now—took his boss's remark closer to heart than my asking him for a beer. I gathered that money had changed hands on the subject of my identity, and possibly on that foul ball.

"I saw your picture when that NSA thing broke last year," Yale said. "You can't buy advertising like that. Make out much, did you?"

"A little. I was up to my chin in conspiracy theorists for a month. Mostly my file in Washington got a little thicker. I may find out what's in it next time I try to book a flight at Metro."

He held a barrel glass in his left hand. Ice cubes rattled in golden liquid when he gestured with it. The bartender, a young black man in a pleated white shirt and leatherette bow tie, broke from the caterers to take command of a bar built into the only wall that didn't have a window. "Your pleasure, sir?"

"I'll drink what Mr. Yale is drinking."

"Eagle Rare." A silver scoop smashed into a sink filled with ice.

When I had my drink I accepted Yale's invitation to join him in a casual conference area made up of sling leather chairs upholstered in the down from some endangered variety of fowl. Gabe stood planted in his spot. His suit jacket was tailored to accommodate his shoulder rig, but the material stretched stiffly across it when he folded his hands behind his back.

Down on the field, an Indian slammed a drive along the third-base line and two Tigers plunged for it, all in eerie silence behind two inches of glass. Someone had turned off the speaker to the announcer's booth. I should've been flattered. I'm not often the center of attention when two of the oldest rivals in baseball are fighting for a spot in the post-season.

Yale either read my mind or had mastered the art of appearing as if he had. "I follow hockey myself; but when I'm in town it pays to be seen at all the local points of interest. Some of the local pillars of society are itching to get out of steel and into fiber optics; they just discovered it, along with the Pacific Ocean. I'm hoping to be in on the garage sale."

"Not aluminum?"

"Sold all mine to China the minute Ford announced the new F-150. I made a profit, and so did the Chinese when they turned around and sold it to Ford. I've gotten to where I am by dumping something just *before* it gets hot."

I didn't have an argument for that. I was barely following the conversation. He asked what had brought me to the city on the lake.

"I came to buy aluminum, but I'm rethinking that now."

He laughed, a short, sharp bark; it seemed to surprise him, like an unexpected hiccup. Gabe scowled—at me, not at his employer. There was less to the bodyguard than met the eye.

I sipped bourbon. It's not my drink, but it was a premium label, and I come from humble origins; you don't waste food or good liquor. I waited for the meeting to come to some kind of point.

Yale worked his mentalist's trick, watching me from beneath half-shuttered lids. "Working on anything at the moment?"

"I just closed out a job. This was meant to be part of my vacation."

"What would it take to persuade you to postpone it?"

"Pig in a poke, Mr. Yale. What would it take to make me earn it?"

"Gabe."

The man in the black suit stepped over and slid a slim tablet in a silver case from a saddle pocket. Plainly they'd dress-rehearsed this since my fifteen seconds of fame had run out. Yale took it, exercised his thumbs, and turned the screen to face me.

The video was silent, but closed-captioned. I recognized the state-of-the-Edwardian-art oak furnishings of a courtroom in the Frank Murphy Hall of Justice in Detroit, perhaps one I'd appeared in myself during one of my occasional arraignments. A thirtyish defendant stood in shirtsleeves with his hands folded in front of him, listening to a judge granting his lawyer's request to release him on bail on a charge of manslaughter, pending sentencing on a guilty plea. It ended abruptly on the young man's back leaving the room.

Yale gave back the tablet without bothering to turn it off. Gabe did that and returned it to his pocket.

"Know him?" Yale said.

I shook my head.

"No reason you should. Cases like that come up all the time. This one's special. That piece of shit you just saw walking out of a court of law murdered my son."

THREE

The Tigers mounted a rally in the top of the ninth. There were players on first and second with two outs. I watched the windup, pretending to consider what Emmett Yale had told me of his son's death.

Detroit leads the nation in felonies involving automobiles. We invented carjacking; the Michigan State Police issue a list of the top-ten most frequently stolen makes and models as regularly as box scores; and we'd been experiencing a fresh run of freeway shootings since spring. Most of them involved road rage incidents that ten years ago would have finished with an exchange of impolite hand signals or at worst a fistfight on the shoulder of the highway. Now, many of them involved running dogfights at eighty miles per hour and amateur snipers potting at whizzing vehicles from convenient overpasses. Lloyd Lipton had been a victim of one of those in August.

"My stepson, actually," Yale said. "My wife's boy, from her first marriage. That's why my name hasn't appeared. The police know it, but they haven't released that information to the press; a courtesy, because I donated a fleet of experimental models to the department last year. They weren't the driverless units we've been having some trouble with."

He sat forward in his chair, rolling his glass between his palms.

"I was advised by my attorney not to go public, as it might prejudice the case in favor of the defendant. You always hear there's one law for the rich and another for everyone else. That's very true, only not the way it's usually meant. I can't even sue some son of a bitch for slandering me, because I'm a public figure, and therefore have no legal right to privacy. Look it up and tell me it's not true."

Cleveland's first baseman caught an easy pop-up and the game was over. Those fans who'd lingered in the aisles to watch the play resumed their exodus, joined by the diehards in the stands.

"Every system's rigged," I said, "but not necessarily against you specifically. Manslaughter's not unusual in this kind of shooting."

"It is when it's premeditated."

I sat back, waiting for him to make his case. There was no use anyway trying to get out of the parking lot for another hour.

Yale spoke in an even but not droning tone, laying out his facts as if he were making a PowerPoint presentation to a board of directors.

Detroit loves automobiles, its climate not so much. The owners of pampered vintage cars have only a narrow window each year— April to November, same as Great Lakes shipping—to show off their investment without exposing thousands of dollars in polished sheet metal and freshly restored chrome to the hazards of black ice, corrosive salt, and potholes as big as crop circles. The August Woodward Dream Cruise lets them do that in a six-hour parade past patient crowds that gather on both sides of the street beginning at dawn. Gunboat-size DeSotos, black-box Model T's, finny Cadillacs, hot-rod Chevies, Buck Rogers Mercs, '60s muscle; every scrap of industry history that had chugged, sputtered, roared, and wolf-whistled its way across most of the twentieth century crawl down the broad main street all morning, squawking horns, popping clutches, boiling over in the heat, and lousing up traffic twenty miles in every direction. The phrase "hell on wheels" might have been coined just for the event.

Lipton, forty-two, was on his way home from it when a bullet fired from an overpass smashed through the windshield of his classic sports car and exploded his skull.

I remembered the story. Except for the Dream Cruise connection, the incident might have been swamped in the general play of freeway shootings that come up on the local news as often as a department store closing. Woodward Avenue, the city's main stem, would have taken Lipton directly to his house in St. Clair Shores, but traffic was at a standstill in all lanes. He pleaded, cursed, and fought his way onto the ramp to I-75 North, but that was almost as bad. The traffic moved in lockstep as far as the zoo, where it set like clay. There he sat for fifteen minutes, pumping toxins into the atmosphere along with everyone else between the tall concrete walls that flank the expressway; and there he sat leaking blood and gray matter into his brown-and-cream upholstery for thirty minutes more, until an ambulance and a tow truck got through the press to clean up the mess. By the time the investigative team reached the overpass—which was clogged like every other local artery—the shooter was long gone.

A combination of surveillance-camera footage, eyewitness reports, and old-fashioned door-to-door interviews turned up a suspect in less than seventy-two hours. Melvin Weatherall—the owner of the pallid face in Yale's video—had dropped out of high school to graduate from the Boys' Training School in Whitmore Lake, a reform institution for juvenile delinquents, and finished his post-graduate degree in the Michigan State Penitentiary in Marquette. His sheet included grand theft auto, home invasion, and a breaking-and-entering beef that emptied a storage building of twenty-two thousand dollars in handguns, rifles, and automatic weapons, one of which was traced to a drive-by shooting that took place later, where the only victims were several plate-glass windows and a phone booth that had been out of order since Desert Storm.

A judge had sentenced him to life as a repeat offender, but an appeals court had sprung him because he was underage at the time of the break-in; that voided any connection to that shooting, which might have been done by another party who had bought the arsenal off the local market after Weatherall disposed of it. To all intents and purposes that made what happened to Lipton a first offense. His attorney succeeded in pleading the charge down from first- to second-degree manslaughter. The prosecutor had gone along with that, but pitched a fit in favor of holding him on a hundred-thousand dollars bail, which the judge refused to order. Weatherall walked the day of Lloyd Lipton's private memorial service.

"It's not unusual," I said again. "It's not right, either. But what makes it Murder One?"

He'd stopped rotating the glass; it wasn't getting any longer for all the kneading. He straightened up and set it on the table at his elbow, a miracle of modern engineering with no visible means of support; spread his hands in the attitude of a lawyer making his summation before a jury.

"No other shots were reported," he said, "no other vehicles hit. Why was he the only one targeted?"

I let his good bourbon pool in the back of my throat before committing it to my stomach; the interview was winding down, and I wasn't likely to taste anything like it for a while. I propped the glass on my thigh, where the thick weighted bottom held it in place like a suction cup.

"Most of these types of shootings don't go on very long. This isn't the kind of lunatic who climbs towers and picks off random targets like Whac-A-Mole until he either gets caught or puts a slug in his own head. More often than sometimes he stepped up from mailbox baseball to something more serious, got scared right away, and skedaddled, whether he hit anything important or not. It doesn't make him any less an animal, but it doesn't make him Charles Manson either."

"So he just happened to be on that overpass," Yale said, "with the traffic inching along below at between zero and ten miles an hour, chose that car at random at that moment, then packed up and left without picking another target?"

"The cops don't sling around 'random' without giving it a lot of consideration. It puts people in a panic. If they thought there was anything to what you suspect, that Lipton was the one and only intended victim, they'd have put it out there right away."

"But that particular car?"

"If the press got it right, it was a mint-condition 1963 Corvette Stingray, sapphire blue with white inserts in the fender panels. It was designed to attract attention. By comparison, four lanes of aerodynamically approved cough drops on wheels would be invisible. If I had a screw loose I'd be tempted myself."

The bodyguard made a noise in his throat. Yale hitched a shoulder. "I'm with Gabe. Do you consider this a joking matter?"

"No, sir. I'm just trying to spare you unnecessary grief. Killings like this fall under the category of a natural disaster. Hurricanes and tornadoes are tragedies. Treating them like there's some kind of evil intelligence behind them just makes things worse."

He picked up his glass, brought it to his lips, then slammed it back down hard enough to slosh three lozenge-shaped pieces of ice over the side. "Damn it, I've spent less time trying to talk people into spending money than you have trying to talk me out of it. Is this some kind of negotiating strategy I'm not aware of?"

"Not at all, Mr. Yale. The money I earned on this trip was spent before I left Detroit. Maybe if you told me the reason why you think your stepson was tagged for a murder victim—the real reason—I'd have a foothold that would help me climb that wall and put his killer in a cell instead of three years' probation and a thousand hours of community service."

Emmett Yale seemed to be aware suddenly that there were more than three people in the room. He cast a glance toward the bartender busying himself with his pourers and siphons, the two women caterers poking around crustaceans and asparagus rolls in the warming trays—not eavesdropping at all, sir, perish the thought—and flicked open a fist the bodyguard's way.

The man in the black suit peeled bills off a saddle he took from his pocket and passed them around. In five minutes the burners were shut off, the perishables packed up, serving tables folded into neat rolling cubes, and Yale, Gabe, and I were left alone with all the liquor in the world. I got up and helped myself to two inches of MacPhail's Centenary. My detective's instincts told me the rest of this meeting was going to call for single malt, neat.

FOUR

hat wasn't really necessary," Yale said, inclining his sleek head toward the door the staff had gone out through. "I paid them to play deaf and dumb and keep it that way. Still."

I held my glass the way they teach you to handle good Scotch, cradling it in my palm. I didn't sit back down. "What happens if they forget?"

Gabe said, "They pay it back."

I looked at him, at the small eyes set deep under the shelf of his brow. Any light that went into them never came back out. Celebrity security is trained to blend with the wallpaper; this one had missed that session. A man like his employer, who'd elbowed his way up practically from the factory floor, wouldn't go to any of the standard agencies to hire protection. In our town you don't build a nuts-and-bolts business bare-handed without taking your share of meetings in pool halls and frozen food lockers and the back rooms of barbershops.

Yale looked down at the dregs in his glass and held it out for the other man to take. Gabe dumped it out into the sink and re-filled it from the same bottle I'd used. He did all this with his left hand; the harness under his coat was a right-hand rig, and would be engineered for speed.

"Now you know what it is I want," Yale said when he had his drink. "Tell me why you're the one to get it for me."

I sipped; shook my head. "I don't bother with questions the other party already knows the answer to."

"Now you sound like a lawyer, and I go through those like Q-tips; *their* investigators, too. The kind they use, I can't tell the difference."

"That's because they spend all their time in libraries and on the phone, farming out their work to other agencies who spend all their time in libraries and on the phone. You didn't just pick me out of the crowd because I was too slow to catch a souvenir ball and not fast enough to duck a camera. You did your homework after you found out my connection with the Hunt case, along with some other likely candidates, put the most promising ones in a basket, and shook it. If I hadn't decided at the last minute to catch a ball game, it might have been any one of the others; or maybe me, with or without the huge hand of fate. You're the Calvinist in the room, I'm not." That was a shot in the dark, but it hit dead center.

"I won't say my faith can't be shaken," he said. "These last couple of years have been an education."

"Most of them are. You know I don't have to charge extra for my silence; that's a package deal, comes with the five hundred a day I charge for mileage and getting broken bones set. The fact that you didn't chivvy me out the door with the rest of the help says you sized me up and decided I'm as good as my advertising." I grinned. "It doesn't really matter to me how much more time you waste. I've been charging you since you started your pitch, so it's up to you if next year's car costs twice as much as the one in the showroom now for no good reason."

"You'll have a sweet time collecting," he said. "I didn't sign anything."

"You got the State Department to waive the tariff on shipping natural gas out of Bolivia on a handshake," I said. "We can't have too many friends in South America. That's not privileged information. My dentist let his subscription to *Sports Illustrated* lapse, so I was stuck with *Forbes*. Don't try to sell me on how unscrupulous you are, Mr. Yale. I do my homework too."

"I can get all the natural gas I need from American cows. You won't find a liter of it in my warehouses. When the loyal opposition raised a ruckus over that piece in *Forbes,* they found there was no evidence to investigate, because no deal was made. My people arranged that meeting and placed the story to drive down the price of oil. But you're fundamentally right. Sit down—unless you're one of those drinkers who's afraid of falling on his face when he tries to stand up."

I sat back down. It was nothing to me if he wanted to think I'm the kind who can't resist a dare.

"Are you a family man, Walker?"

"No."

"You dodged a bullet. I met Lloyd too late to have any real influence on how he turned out. The man was already set in the mold; I was born and raised in Grand Rapids, and there's no escaping the lessons of the Dutch Reformed Church. I tried to give him work, but the concept of showing up at the same time every day and staying there for eight hours was alien to his nature. I won't go into the fights we had, the blow-by-blow. In the end it was simpler just to put him on a fixed allowance and let him live at home. The house is big enough we wouldn't have to go through a rematch every time we met in a hallway. I did insist on a family dinner at least once a week, as long as he was under my roof. I owed his mother that much in the way of a show of old-fashioned domesticity. That turned out to be a mistake, because I fell for it myself, and let my business seep into the conversation."

I tapped out a cigarette, held it up. He opened his fist in that same impatient gesture, only with a different meaning. His silent vocabulary was broader than his speech. A skull-crusher of a glass ashtray appeared at my elbow; I was barely aware Gabe had left his station. A man that light on his feet would have done his share of damage in a pair of trunks. I made another note, to look up his record. We weren't getting along as well as I'd like. I dropped my match into the tray and watched the smoke drift toward the AC exhaust.

"Little pitchers have big ears," I said. "What was it, the gas deal? Oh, right; there wasn't any. You'll have to bear with me. I never draw a Get out of Jail card when I play Monopoly."

"It was computer chips. I cornered the market one week before the supply gave out. I guess you could say I'm partially responsible for the shortage." He swallowed Scotch. "I'm relying on that advertising of yours, Walker. Anti-trust would admire to add my scalp to their string, and Ford, GM, and Honda would admire to make it even more worth their while."

I said, "That horse is dead or you wouldn't be beating it in front of a stranger. Made a bundle, did he?" I almost said, *made a killing.*

"He could've made more, if he'd invested directly in the Silicon Valley interests I went to, instead of selling the information for a flat fee. I think I was angrier about that than I was about the insider trading. I dislike a crook, but I detest a stupid one."

I smoked; said nothing. I was beginning to get the drift.

"My stepson had extravagant tastes," he said. "His father indulged them. He was an investment banker, and I suppose it was easier to bribe his son to avoid distraction from his juggling act between New York and Tokyo and Switzerland. He made Lloyd the gift of that money drain of a Corvette as compensation for leaving him and his mother. I wish I could say it was the most expensive of his vices." He was watching me from under his sleepy lids. I wondered if that came from practice or if it was what determined the course of a man's life as far back as the crib. "I'm getting the impression I won't have to spell out why I can't be connected with this matter in public."

"I see more than that," I said. "The Securities and Exchange Commission has no case against you for trading confidential information; only Lloyd could provide that link."

The lids snapped up; I could almost hear them flapping on the roll. "Hold on! I—"

"Of course not." I didn't even want to look at Gabe; he was breathing audibly, like a bull snorting and pawing earth. "He's your wife's son. What I was getting at is if it leaks out Lloyd was shady, Weatherall's defense will use it to paint the victim as black as possible and get his killer an even sweeter deal, maybe even an acquittal."

He slipped back into partial hibernation. Just for a moment, though, I'd seen what his defeated competitors had failed to until it was too late. He looked at his watch, a simple one in a steel case on a leather strap. "What do I owe you so far?"

"Nothing. That was a just a test, to see if you'd squawk. Rich people who squeeze every buck like a pimple are no fun to work for."

"Your work's fun?"

"If I didn't like it I wouldn't put up with the parts I don't. But enough about me. Who bought the information?"

"Does it matter?"

"You know damn well it does."

"Okay," he said. "I had to know how much rope I had to pay out before you knew where to grab; that was part of the test. If Clare Strickling didn't put Weatherall on that overpass, it happened the way the judge saw it, and I can't swallow that. No one else had a solid reason to take Lloyd out of the rotation. Strickling knew the boy as well as I did, and that if the SEC got to him and applied pressure, he'd fold like a card table and give him up."

"Clare's a man?"

"Clare's a hyena. He was Clarence in his personnel file, but that pretty face of his didn't light up when anyone called him by it."

"He worked for you?"

"Until a member of Gabe's security unit caught him trying to smuggle spec sheets out of Research and Development. An ad flack had no reason even being on that floor. Last year's Lexus bore a closer than coincidental resemblance to this year's Yale; that's when I replaced my security head with Gabe. I didn't have to go to Accounting to add two and two. Strickling thought I was bluffing when I threatened to have him arrested for industrial espionage—he said it was a bad publicity risk—but at that point I had nothing to hide and I knew my business would survive.

"Well, now is now, but then was then. I was on the phone to Legal when he agreed to fold his tent and steal away. Emphasis on steal." He emptied his glass. A set of strong jaws crunched ice. "I might have been the bigger man. I wasn't. I had Gabe shot-put him down the front steps, messed up his classic profile. So that gave him a personal reason to target my legal heir on top of staying out of Club Fed."

"Where can I find him?"

"Hang on." He unclenched his free hand again, but if there was any difference in the way it was done this time I didn't see it. The bodyguard passed over the silver tablet.

Yale's fingers were long and slim, unlike the rest of him. Once a draftsman, always a draftsman: Constant tinkering with mechanical pencils had kept them trim. He turned the screen my way. The numbers he'd typed out might have been the elevation of a High Plains state.

"Give me your routing number—if we've come to an understanding—and that will be deposited in your account before your bank closes today."

FIVE

The usual assortment of candy-corn traffic cones, deserted equipment, lane shifts, and no sign of any construction going on during the drive home gave me plenty of time to work out a plan of attack.

Emmett Yale was expecting me to brace Clare Strickling right away, but there were a dozen good reasons not to do that. The most important was that it *was* what the client expected me to do; and if *he* did, so would Strickling. I could practically write the scenario of that meeting, with all the cues and pickups in place. There was no fun in that; better to leave the suspect waiting, second-guessing all his answers until they played even to him like a third-rate lounge act covering the hits of Tom Jones. That was when they tripped over their own tongues. The plan I came up with was no less risky given the situation—worse, because it put my professional future in hock—but it promised more entertainment. I like my job most of the time.

The only lights still on when I turned into my block belonged to those neighbors who ate when they were hungry, slept when they were sleepy, and remembered a time when there was always something worth watching on television; the place got noisy only on weekends, when the grandkids came to visit. In the garage I spread what was left of Fred Dowling's topcoat over the lawn mower to protect it from dust, then threw some leftover chicken between two slices of bread in the kitchen and ate it in the breakfast nook with a beer. Then I went to bed for the first time all year with enough money in the bank to sleep without one eye open for collection agencies.

I lingered over breakfast, then dressed in a suit without green-and-white checks, a tie that wasn't hand-painted at the state fair, and shoes that didn't come to a point; where I was going, I didn't want to be mistaken for a bail bondsman.

There was no reason to hurry. Jurors are told to register at eight A.M. and the judges seldom get in before ten. The one I wanted was more conscientious than most, but something told me it was best not to barge into his chambers until after he'd had a chance to settle in and put on his game face.

The Frank Murphy Hall of Justice stands at the corner of Beaubien and Gratiot, a tall pile of combed concrete as faceless as justice itself, with a bronze-and-granite *non sequitur* of a statue of a naked man standing in the palm of an amputated hand on a two-story pedestal out front; a puzzle of some kind that everyone who goes there is too involved in his own affairs to take time to figure out. Inside is the standard labyrinth of polished corridors, clerks' stations behind bulletproof glass, shysters in wash-and-wear suits passing out business cards on every corner like handbills, and disgruntled cops polishing benches outside closed double doors in their Sunday clothes, waiting to give testimony on their day off. The custodial staff buffs the floors every evening, and until the following noon when the flop sweat takes over, the place smells like the first day of school.

In contrast to the lower floors where the courtrooms are, the upper stories are so quiet you can hear a bailiff turning pages in *National Geographic* in a lavatory on the other side of the building. My footsteps followed me out of the elevator and down a hall walled in marble to a door with J GALE KITCHNER lettered in gold on black walnut. I knocked on it gently; those surroundings call for whispers and hushed anticipation. A voice that sounded like a throat being cleared invited me to enter.

What the architecture of the late sixties lacked in inspiration it more than made up for in judges' chambers. The room was a perfect cube, paneled in more walnut, with an old-fashioned bowl of heavy opalescent glass hanging in chains from the ceiling. A rug bordered in a Greek key design covered the polished floor to within two feet of the walls and a semicircle of oak-and-leather captain's chairs faced a desk carved out of timbers from the original Ark. The room had the deep-finish musk of an English gentlemen's club: mulled wine, cured tobacco, smoky heather, and old books.

In the middle of all this, in a tufted horsehide swivel with a high curved back, sat the man the decorator had had in mind as he was sorting through his swatches and paint chips. J Gale Kitchner—the J came without a period, because it stood for nothing, apart from an ear for rhythm and cadence—wore a shirt with garnet cuff links with BLIND JUSTICE embossed on them in gold (a gift upon his retirement from private practice), a black butterfly tie with the corners tucked out of sight behind the collar, and a shock of hair like a white flame. Even when sitting, he was a tall old length of string, high-shouldered, with bright bird's eyes glittering far back under thistled brows and a chin you could use to pound rivets. An Army Colt .45 semiautomatic with hickory grips rested on top of a stack of files next to the blotter. It wasn't a paperweight; Detroit Recorder's Court had been disbanded, but the judges who had presided over it still led the nation's court system in death threats.

"I have a trial in twenty minutes," he said in that phlegmy voice. "State your business."

"Amos Walker, your honor." I showed him the license in its folder, keeping the meaningless deputy's star turned back out of sight. "I need information on an arraignment you heard recently. It won't take twenty minutes."

He tipped his snowy thatch at the captain's chairs. I took the one in the center.

He sat back, resting a glittering cuff on the desk. "Been behaving yourself?"

I grinned. "I wasn't sure you'd remember me."

"I remember the cocky ones and the mousy ones mostly. All the rest are like the memorial services I've attended. The guests of honor come and go, and nothing ever seems to change. But when I chance to read a newspaper and someone I once dropped the gavel on is in it, I take notice. Especially when he shows up more than once. You're in danger of becoming a celebrity."

"What's fifteen minutes out of a lifetime?" I shook my head. "I wasn't cocky; just resigned. When I don't have anything to trade the cops in return for a pass, there's nothing for it but to leave things to the man in charge. At least with you I knew I'd get an even break."

"Stow the saddle soap, Walker. What was privileged communication yesterday may be privileged communication tomorrow, but today it could just as well be obstruction of justice. The law's slick as an eel and I've made too many compromises to confuse horseshit with roses. Why are you here?"

"I saw you in a video presiding over Melvin Weatherall's arraignment. I want to ask how much you know about the case."

"He pled guilty. The gun was never found. He could have taken his chances with a jury, but he was genuinely remorseful. When you've seen as much of the other kind as I have, you learn to recognize the real thing when it's in front of you. He was drunk or high on meth and pills—his words, so I was inclined in that direction, although the results of the blood draw were moot after a delay of several hours—and bore no malice. I split the difference between Man One and Two, ran the bail amount up the middle, and put him on a tether. He made bond on a ten-percent surety and now there's a vacant cell waiting for some pig who tied his wife to a radiator and beat her into a coma or some piece of shit who took a shot at a competing dealer and killed a four-year-old girl riding in the back seat. So if you're working for the Libertarian Party looking to connect me to undeclared income in Switzerland, tell 'em I was too busy counting euros to give you the time."

"I'm working for Emmett Yale."

He shifted his weight in his chair. The face he made wasn't surprise or disapproval. I remembered he'd had an encounter with a punji stick while leading a patrol in Khe Sanh and that was why he didn't have children. "That would've been my next guess."

"You knew he was Lloyd Lipton's stepfather?"

"Don't pretend you're surprised. You came to me because the judge in any case knows more about it than anyone in the jury pool. Your next question is did Yale's connection with the victim influence my decision; in which case I'll declare court in session right here in chambers and jail you for contempt."

This time I tamped down my grin. "Judge Del Rio did that in Detroit Police Headquarters. It wasn't long after that he was almost killed in the crossfire during the shootout in his courtroom."

"Detroit was different then; and unlike Del Rio, I was taught to return fire." He skinned back a cuff, looked at his watch. "Eleven minutes. Five of which I spend doing breathing exercises before I robe up." Tiny bright eyes fixed on the bridge of my nose, hard as steel pellets.

"I want to interview Weatherall. Where does he live?"

"Your client has the resources to find that out for you. Why come to me?"

"He wants to stay out of it as much as possible. If the press gets word he's involved, they may turn the tide of public opinion Weatherall's way, the rich being parasites sucking the blood of the proletariat when they're not all out foxhunting; get him off with a fine and time served. Which is what, twelve hours?"

"If you take what you learn to another judge and get my decision reversed, I'm a mollycoddle. Why should I do that?"

"Because you're not; and if you refuse me a piece of information that's not privileged, it means you're afraid of the tag, which would make you worse than a mollycoddle. If there's anything the public hates more than a fat cat, it's abuse of power. Your honor," I added.

He'd been behind the bench too long—and in front of it even longer—to show anything like emotion in the face of a threat a lot less mild than the one I'd suggested. He snatched a ballpoint pen out of the onyx set on the desk, scribbled something on a pad, tore off a sheet, and stuck it out. "Take that to Mrs. Feeney down the hall. It's the only room where the door's always open. She'll be in touch.

"One thing." He snatched back the sheet as I was reaching for it. "I'm retiring next March. Take the advice of an old mouthpiece and don't bend any laws before then. Because I'll move planets to make sure whatever you did falls under my jurisdiction."

SIX

The door near the end of the corridor stood open as advertised. A small, plump woman wearing a black wig with a fillip at the bottom redirected her gaze from a computer screen to Kitchner's note, then a business card that told no lies about me, and said she'd call when she had what I wanted. The trivet on her desk said she was Mrs. L. Feeney.

In the blue zone in front of 1300 I cranked my Cutlass out from between a gridded-glass Corrections Department van and a bar of silver-colored soap on wheels—probably one of the unmarked units Emmett Yale had given the police—and took the John Lodge up to I-94 West.

The city of Saline lies forty-five minutes from Detroit, if you take the speed-limit signs as a suggestion only, a privilege of our particular metropolitan area. It's an Ann Arbor suburb that's big enough to claim suburbs of its own, hanging on with all four limbs and its teeth to the small-town image that Ann Arbor gave up long ago, with a respectable amount of greensward and a business district that's still recognizable from the horse-and-buggy photos that hang on the walls of many of its buildings. Yale Mobility's headquarters was there, in a sprawl of new construction resembling a college campus, and also the proving track where it worked the bugs out of its finished product on the old county fairgrounds. An eighteen-foot-high yellow sound-retention wall shielded the neighboring housing developments from the noise of the test vehicles—somewhat muted now by electrical engineering, but loud enough still to spoil backyard barbecues. If Yale's personnel file was still up to date as to where Clare Strickling lived, I'd find him in a fairly new apartment complex on the state road.

I could have phoned, and saved myself the trip if he'd moved out, but I didn't want to put him on alert and take the chance of having to slash my way through a briar patch of lawyers to get to him. If it didn't pan out I could lunch at Zingerman's deli in Ann Arbor and charge a Reuben on a homemade roll to my client.

The complex was laid out in twin rows of three-story brick buildings separated by dogwalks with exposed staircases leading to the upper floors. It was a pleasant middle-class family place with a country feel, the way they still like things in places like Saline. There was a retention pond in back with ducks floating on it like wooden decoys and playground equipment made of molded plastic standing on a rubber mat; but any kid could rack up all the cuts and scrapes he wanted on the sidewalk that ringed the pond.

It was nice enough, but Strickling could do better, if what Yale had told me about his stock deal held water.

His was a second-story unit halfway down from the entrance to the lot. Before I left the car I popped open the glove compartment and took the .38 Chief's Special in its holster from behind the Judas flap and clipped it to my belt. I hadn't needed it for the Dowling case; embezzlers as a rule don't pack anything more lethal than pocket calculators. A dead man with a bullet in his brain was a different dynamic.

It was a corner room on the second floor with a brief balcony overhanging the parking lot and a screw-you hole in the door. An eye came to it at my knock. I swept my ID folder past it, enough to flash the tin star but not enough to read the cheaply embossed lettering. Something snapped and the door came open just wide enough to stretch the security chain.

Yale had said Strickling had a pretty face. The half I saw was pleasantly arranged, with a high cheekbone, a straight nose, a full lower lip, and a chin you just knew was cleft right where the edge of the door caught it. The lashes were long and had a silken sheen. The nose was chopped off square at the tip, but on that face it wasn't so much a flaw as the last-minute decision of a sculptor who liked plane geometry. I made the same abrupt choice and clocked him at thirty-five.

"I'm Strickling," he said when I asked. "Let's have a better look at that badge."

"It doesn't improve on closer inspection. I got it twenty years ago to serve papers with and they forgot to ask for it back. The name's Walker. I'm a Michigan State–licensed investigator."

"A license doesn't mean you work for Lansing. What's it about?"

"Something you probably don't want your neighbors listening in on." I leaned in close and whispered, "Lloyd Lipton."

If that panicked him it only showed on the part of his face I couldn't see. But he closed the door long enough to unhook the chain and opened it wide.

I had two inches on him vertically, but his shoulders were disproportionately broad, giving him a top-heavy look, reinforced by the way he stood, with his brown feet spread in flip-flops and his knees bent slightly to keep them from locking at the joints. He wore a black T-shirt with a telltale rectangle rolled up in one sleeve and shorts, and his bare brown legs and bare brown arms were knobby-muscled from squats and pull-ups. His hair was a dark haze, buzzed close enough to the scalp to show the ridges where the parts of his skull joined. The cut, and the gnarled limbs, suggested a conscious attempt to compensate for his womanish good looks; then again, that might have been too much to get from a first glimpse. Detectives can be as impressionable as anyone else.

"Yale sent you."

It wasn't a question, so I slid in around him without answering. The living room was carpeted in gray, with muted lilac walls, an overhead fixture with a fake Tiffany shade, matching taupe sofa and armchairs, and a pair of glass-topped end tables. It had as much personality as an Ikea display. An eggshell-colored aluminum suitcase was spread open on the sofa, half-filled, with a stack of folded shirts on the cushion beside it.

"Moving," I said. "I don't blame you. Digs like these can overstimulate the heart."

"I had the place three years and I doubt I spent more than a couple of weeks in it all told," he said. "Yale had a YMCA setup at the office so he could get sixteen hours a day out of his executive staff. Just temporary, he told us, till we're off the ground. Give your soul to God and thou shalt have treasures in heaven. Only when everything was up and running he found ways to shove us overboard."

"Us? I heard he set you adrift in a one-man lifeboat for insider trading."

That didn't put him any more on the defensive than dropping Lipton's name. He glanced at his watch, a gaudy thing of platinum and red gold that told the time in twelve zones. "I barely knew Lipton well enough to say hello to; and I probably wouldn't have bothered even with that if he weren't the boss's stepson. He sure never gave me inside dope on what the old man was buying. That was Yale's excuse to can me along with all the executive staff so he could replace us with entry-level help. He built the place on our backs."

"Report it to the union?"

"What union? That's for the salaried employees. We all had contracts. Fat lot of good those are when it's the big cheese's lawyers who draw them up. No class-action outfit would take the case. Their pockets aren't deep enough to take on an outfit that size.

"I'm not Gordon Gekko," he went on. "My broker advised me that the company I invested in was an up-and-comer. I didn't make out anything like Rockefeller on the deal. It was already almost too rich for my blood by the time I jumped on it. Know what I think? I think there weren't enough Dutch boys in the world to stop up all the holes in that dike. Ask Svenson and Brill, my investment counselors. They'll tell you nobody cleared dick when the closing bell rang. If I had bought anything from Lipton, it made me more goose than crook. So you've got revenge for a bullshit motive if the first doesn't work out."

"Can we sit?"

"Sure. You want a drink too? Had breakfast? I can send out."

I let that float past and helped myself to an armchair. Rising to sarcasm is the privilege of youth.

He dumped the stack of shirts into the suitcase and sat on the end of the sofa, taking another peek at his watch as he did so.

"Know what *I* think?" I said. "I think not making enough on the deal to buy anything more than a flashy wristwatch and maybe a marginally better place to relocate is no defense against the watchdogs who work for the SEC. Ever say hello to Melvin Weatherall?"

He almost looked at the watch again, then thought about whether or not to get mad; decided to play it casual.

"I wondered when we'd come around to that. Yale couldn't prove I did anything wrong in the market, or he'd have had me prosecuted, and he doesn't have the guts to accuse me of anything else—homicide, say—so he farmed it out. Handling it himself would tip his hand, open him up to a lawsuit for slander and malicious prosecution; which is why I'm talking to you instead of that goon Gabe Parrish. I guess what I saved on not popping for a

Harvard attorney when he fired me without cause would pay for a hit man."

He hadn't smiled before, and I saw why. His long teeth and too much gum line spoiled his good looks. "Murder, seriously? To shield me from a white-collar rap I could beat standing on one foot? He's slipping worse than I thought."

"I just asked if you knew Weatherall. It wasn't an essay question."

"Then no. It's not likely we'd run into each other. I don't hang out in tattoo parlors or go to monster truck rallies. Yeah," he said, nodding, "I keep up on the local news. His kind breed like rats." He checked the time again, this time making sure I saw it.

I went on before he could tell me he had a softball game to get to. I was beginning to wonder what I was keeping him from.

"It's just routine, Mr. Strickling. The wheels of justice don't grind small enough for men like Emmett Yale. If they did I'd be looking for a job myself. Any prospects?"

"I have, as a matter of fact. I—"

I interrupted. "Not my business. I'm just making small talk. What exactly was your job description?"

"Research and Development, same as his when he started out. I designed this year's model."

"The one under investigation?"

"'Observation.' And I wasn't responsible for the bugs coming off the line. I told Yale the prototype wasn't ready for the market. He pushed it through anyway. Frankly, I was surprised when he canned me for suspicion of insider trading. I thought he'd keep me around long enough to lay the complaints off on me. I'll bet he's kicking himself for not thinking of that when he had the chance."

He was talking faster now, not really paying attention to what he was saying.

A couple of filtered butts occupied a plain copper ashtray on the table next to the sofa. I was a rude guest. I tapped one out of my pack and set fire to it without asking.

The handsome face pulled taut. He started to raise his wrist again; changed directions and unrolled a pack of Pall Malls and a book of matches from his sleeve. He shook out the flame, flipped the match into the tray, and blew a stuttering jet of smoke toward a corner of the ceiling.

I said, "I'll have that drink now. Thanks for offering."

He coughed, took the cigarette from between his lips, and fanned away smoke. He was doing a lousy job of showing he had all the time in the world to sit around drinking a hole in the morning. "All I've got is sherry." He made it sound like liver and onions.

"Fine."

A small kitchen took up part of a hall leading to the back of the apartment. He got up and took a black bottle from a cupboard. He brought me a narrow stemmed glass with just enough tawny liquid in the bottom to drown a flea. I took it, thanked him, and cradled it in one hand, swished the contents around like Noël Coward. Didn't drink.

He puffed his cigarette down to the letters, put it out in the tray, started to reach again for the pack, didn't, then did. Now he was paying more attention to the door I'd come in through than what time it was. He was so busy not looking at the burning match he just missed setting fire to a finger. I never got so much entertainment out of a glass of liquor I hadn't touched.

"Excuse me," he said, putting out the butt. "I have a call to make."

"Sure." I drained my glass then. The stuff tasted like Mercurochrome. "Mind if I pour myself another?"

He wasn't listening. He snatched a cordless off the end table, carried it down the hall, and shut a door. I wandered out to the kitchen, rinsed out my glass, filled it from the tap, and swished the cloying aftereffects of sherry off my tongue and teeth, spitting into the sink.

They don't make doors like they used to. Down the hall, in a bedroom or something, Strickling was arguing with someone.

"I know, I know. Something came up, okay? I'll meet you. No, not there. You *know* why. Okay. Better give me an hour. Believe me, I know. Okay."

One more "I know," two more "okays," and I was back in my seat, using the empty glass to dump my ashes when he came back carrying the receiver. If I were him I'd have duck-walked me out the door fifteen minutes ago.

He stopped in his tracks. "I've got nothing more to say to you."

I ditched my stub in the glass and left. I didn't go far; just to the end of the parking lot where I'd left my car. The revolver was wearing a hole in my back. I took it off my belt, holster and all, and laid it on the passenger seat. I focused the side mirror on the staircase leading down from the building I'd just left.

A woman in a housecoat came out of a ground-floor apartment to shake dust from a rug, sending brown billows toward the highway. I didn't see anyone else just then, or expect to. Whoever Clare Strickling had been waiting to drop in would be steaming back east; cutting in and out of traffic, hot under the collar, judging by the end of the conversation I'd heard. I guessed east, based on the hour Strickling had bought himself, but as much by instinct. Sooner or later everything comes back to Detroit.

SEVEN

fter ten minutes Strickling came downstairs and out into the parking lot, jiggling keys in his right hand and looking in all directions like a bit player in a spy spoof. He'd changed into street shoes and grown-up slacks and carried a zippered portfolio under one arm covered in forest-green fabric. I reached into the back seat for my field glasses and focused in on the leatherette nameplate on the outside: YALE MOBILITY. I grinned. A man who'd buy inside information from the boss's son wouldn't think twice about lugging around the booty in a stolen company folder; if that's what was in it. Could've been the plans to the invasion of Syria or a set of Ginsu knives.

He cast barely a glance toward the Dumpster, climbed under the wheel of a cranberry-colored Lexus—no company car for this ex-employee—and tickled the motor to grumbling life. He seemed to have found a way to take some of the sting out of being a disappointed stockholder. But he was easy to keep in sight bobbing in the flood of local steel streaming east. We averaged between seventy-five and eighty, which kept us up with the flow. Along that stretch the cops don't stir for anything up to ninety, and not even then when the shift change is in progress.

We nicked the edge of the noon rush, at its heaviest north of downtown, where the office trade goes to eat now that the quieter restaurants in the business corridor have closed; you can't plot a hostile takeover shouting over the TV announcers in the Hockey-town Cafe. Our place in the universe is sectioned off by invisible city walls.

When we exited and turned left on Conner, I had one of those moments of premonition; but then ESP is largely a combination of luck, experience, and blind faith. Just then a sleek blue-and-silver corporate jet came banking into the wind coming off the river, shedding a hundred yards per second as it glided in for a landing, roaring politely, like a dinner guest stifling a belch.

That was a pat on the head for the Great Detective. I was so damn sure of myself I started to slow down before the Lexus as we approached the entrance to Detroit City Airport; a dead giveaway if Strickling were paying attention, but he was too busy reading the signs. It seemed to be his first visit. That wasn't unusual. Wayne County Metropolitan had taken the lead when passenger jets got too big to turn around at City. Now only private pilots, air couriers, and scaled-down business shuttles use the smaller field, to avoid the crush at Metro. Apart from that it's a secret no one bothers to keep.

It was sunny, one of those russet-gold days that con us into thinking autumn will just go on and on and Old Man Winter in his dotage will overlook Michigan this time. I rolled down my window and thought I smelled burning leaves; then I didn't. It was just old cigarette smoke getting out.

The traffic was growing scarce. I fell back a country block, navigating mostly by the Lexus' brake lights when it slowed to take a corner, speeding up a little when it vanished behind a building, then easing off the throttle when I had it back in sight. Strickling hovered around twenty and seemed to be concentrating more on what was in front of him than what was behind. He was going by directions someone had given him. That settled the point. He hadn't been there before.

We passed the entrance; I thought at first he'd missed the sign, which was prominent enough. But he rolled on at the same moderate speed for half a mile, then slowed for the turn through an open gate in a chain-link fence topped with coils of razor wire, Detroit's official flower. It belonged to a private airfield, paved two-thirds of the way back to an area where yellow Caterpillars busied themselves shoving around mounds of raw orange earth, growling and beeping and farting diesel exhaust as they pushed, dragged, flattened, and filled, sculpting semi-civilization out of old Indian territory. A scrum of men in coveralls, hard hats, and one pinstripe suit stood on the edge of the project, wrestling blueprints. The place was under either construction or expansion, probably anticipating annexation to the bigger operation next door.

City is to Metro what a country store is to the Mall of America; this was hardly more than a kiosk. The government hawkeyes inside the long horizontal terminal building up the road had no interest in the plain Quonset-type hangars here, where the traffic-copter pilots, amateur aviators, and local entrepreneurs sheltered their equipment. There'd be surveillance cameras and private security, but not to the degree that they've taken all the fun out of air travel everywhere else.

We took a curving drive to the north end of the airport, passed a string of long low buildings of various sizes, and slowed as we approached a cigar-shaped metallic structure with yard-high letters extending the length of the hip roof:

GOLDEN EAGLE EXCURSIONS

This time when he braked I made a square turn, coasted to a stop in a backwater lot of sub-compacts, extinct sedans, and a lime-green Suburban missing its left taillight assembly—clearly an employee zone—and watched as he slid into a slot ten cars down and got out, the portfolio under his arm. I was growing excited about that item; he was hanging on to it as if it contained the nuclear codes.

The entrance to the building was in front, under a chalky painting of a testy-looking bird of prey with a crew cut and wings spread wall to wall, an eagle uncomfortably like the one carved on the pediment atop the old Reichstag. The door was a slide-up affair made of articulated metal panels. He raised a fist, beat on it, waited, then stepped back as it lifted on chains, clanking and rattling up the tracks loud enough for the noise to reach me.

Strickling stiffened suddenly, backed away two more steps.

In the next second I knew why.

A louder noise from inside the building swamped the clatter of the door; the measured roar of an unmuffled engine. Strickling turned, picked up his pace; lost his balance when loose gravel rolled out from under one foot, almost fell. Twisting to recover his equilibrium, he released his grip on the portfolio, then threw his other arm across his body to catch it in both hands. I couldn't say much for his sense of priority, but he was operating on instinct. Greed can do that to a person, even when his life's at stake.

He was running now, but the race was lost.

Behind him, something came rolling out from inside the hangar on fat inflated tires, pistons thundering loudly enough to shake the ground under the car I was sitting in, pulled along by a propeller spinning too fast to see the blades. It was a four-passenger Piper, painted a crisp red and white, its single wing supported by struts, the sun approaching noon reflecting from the flat angled windows enclosing the cockpit, turning them into sheets of steel so that I couldn't tell if there was anyone in the pilot's seat.

My hands gripped the steering wheel hard enough to split the knuckles. It was as if I thought I could turn the craft away from the running man by remote action.

But even that wouldn't have been fast enough; it had no more chance than Strickling outrunning an accelerating plane with an angry roaring thing whirling up front like a buzz saw. For a moment it looked as if he might make it, but the machine was gaining momentum. When it caught up to him he flung his arms up and wide, the flat portfolio spinning away from his grip, his mouth open far enough to unhinge his jaw; I knew that, because mine was open just as wide and something clicked on both sides.

I was as incapable of motion as a stone stuck in a mudbank. I couldn't turn my head away any more than Strickling could; not even when the propeller struck, splashing blood and brain and shards of polished white skull in every direction.

EIGHT

I was out of the car before he finished falling. The gun was in my hand. I didn't remember snatching it up.

The force of the blow spun Strickling on one foot; that foot was the last to touch ground. He twisted half around, sagged at the waist, and descended slowly as a leaf, landing first on his buttocks and then his back, arms still spread. The red stain on the ground was sunflower-shaped; what was left of his head settled squarely into its center as if it were professionally framed. That stray foot came down, moved convulsively, scraping a ditch in the dirt. After three tries it gave up trying for leverage and stopped.

The plane continued to roll. Out in the open, the corpse behind it, it made a lazy turn, away from the sun so that I could see the cockpit was empty. It bumped over breaks in the asphalt, its engine bawling like a furious baby, slowed when its tires reached a shaggy strip of grass at the edge of the field, and came to a jarring stop against an earthen berm at the base of the chain-link fence, its tailpiece lifting and its propeller churning up black divots the size of Strickling's shattered head, until one of the blades stuck fast and the engine choked and died.

After that the silence went off like a bomb. I shook myself loose of my second stroke of torpor in as many minutes and sprinted toward the hangar, pulled along by the momentum of the

.38. Nearing the open door I cut my pace and edged in around the two-by-four frame, gun first. Forty feet of uninhabited interior beckoned, lit dimly through that opening and a smaller rectangle at the back where an ordinary door swung wide. An aisle of concrete stretched the entire length between two rows of aircraft and aircraft-related items: twin- and single-engine planes, a bubble helicopter stripped of its skin, showing the dinosaur bones of its frame, a rotary engine the size of the Liberty Bell resting on sawhorses. The reek of oil, scorched metal, and fresh bitter exhaust was thick enough to swim in.

I stuck the revolver under my belt in back. Whoever had started that plane toward its victim was long gone.

When I went back out, a crowd had formed around the thing on the ground, with more on its way, running from the direction of other hangars and a trailer up on blocks inside the main gate that would serve as the office. Nobody was paying any attention to me. I wandered over to where Strickling's portfolio had landed and picked it up. I didn't bother to open it there. It was in the back seat of my car by the time the police arrived, noisy as ever. As if there were any hurry.

Inspector John Alderdyce finished with the items in the dead man's wallet, passed it to a uniform for bagging, and stripped off his disposable gloves. They'd played hell with the rest of his ensemble, a medium-weight gray single-breasted, lilac-colored shirt, figured necktie, and shoes polished high black to match his flesh: an *Ebony* cover wrapped around *The Police Gazette*. He nodded to another officer, who replaced the brown canvas tarp an airport employee had provided to cover the corpse.

"Hang around long enough you see everything," Alderdyce said. "I've been with Homicide since I got off Stationary Traffic, and this is the first time I've seen an airplane used as a murder weapon."

I said, "No kidding, you were a meter maid?"

He took that with his usual show of smoldering patience. "I had the legs for the job. What did you see?"

I told him. I already had once, on top of telling it to the first responders from the nearest precinct and a nosy off-duty detective first-grade who'd happened to be in the neighborhood and then happened to be somewhere else when the top brass arrived. There was no reason for me to complain and make the interview that much longer.

"Clare," he said, "what kind of name's that for a man?"

"I didn't know him long enough to call him by it, so I didn't ask. He was what you cops call uncooperative. When he left home right after I interviewed him, I got curious and tagged along behind. I thought I had him figured out until he blew past City Airport. You might catch a twelve-passenger jet there for South America or some other place with enough of a mad on against the U.S. to oppose extradition. This place doesn't have enough runway. Canada, maybe; but why not just drive across the border?"

"Why leave at all? You notice I haven't asked yet what kind of case you're working and for who."

"I did. I admired your restraint." I rolled a shoulder. "I have to ask permission first. You've heard that before. I should have it printed on cards, like the deaf."

"So call."

I was walking away, fishing out my cell, when another motor came blatting around the corner of the hangar. The noise stood my skin on edge; I was off the internal combustion engine for the time being. I pocketed the phone and turned around in time to see a bulbous motorcycle with sausage-shaped saddlebag tanks slalom between crowd-control cops setting up barricades, execute a half-circle as it came near the hangar, and brake to a halt. Blue-gray smoke from the pipes drifted forward and rolled along the ground, shredding when it reached the fence.

The motor fired one pistol-like shot, then went silent. The biker dismounted, unbuckled and removed a teardrop-shaped helmet, and shook loose a bale of chestnut hair.

If she'd wriggled into the jodhpurs, high-topped boots, and brown suede jerkin to mask her sex, she'd missed by a mile. She was a well-tended thirty-five with a wiry build, but not so much I couldn't take her two falls out of three, rested and having taken my vitamins. Her face was oval, with a slightly square chin and high Native American cheekbones; but that image might have been suggested by the legend scripted in white on the near gasoline tank: INDIAN. Her eyelashes were long enough to trap snowflakes.

"Palm Volker, Officer," she said, sticking out a lean hand with spread joints, the fingers of an athlete. "I manage this field."

He wrapped it in his big gnarled fist. "Palm. It's all about names, this one. Maybe I should change mine to Persimmon." He showed her his badge and ID, snapped the folder shut. "Clare Strickling. Know him?"

"No. Is that him?" She tilted her head toward the body. It might have been all tarp for as much effect as it seemed to have on her.

"It was. This man?" He pointed the folder at me as I approached.

A pair of honey-colored eyes inventoried me from crown to heels, then turned his way. "Should I?"

"Ms. Volker, this conversation will be a lot shorter if you'd answer the questions as they come."

"Then no. Did he witness the accident?"

I wasn't there anymore, for Ms. Volker.

"We're not sure it *was* an accident." He pointed the folder again, this time at a surveillance camera mounted under the eave of the hangar. "Does that work?"

She glanced that way. "I hope so. As you can see, we're undergoing a lot of construction. We turn things on, we turn them off; our insurance company frowns on electrocuting personnel. Then there are the interruptions we don't expect, such as inadvertently parting an underground cable. It's a clusterfuck, Lieutenant. Like always."

"Inspector. Any others that might have an angle on this part of the field?"

"I'll have to check. Some of our cameras are cleverly concealed, even from me."

"You've got a trusting boss, don't you?"

"Do you?" She had a tight little smile I liked. "Some of our tenants have cameras of their own. I'll have someone check them out. The FAA might call dibs on anything we get."

"The plane never left the ground."

She made a poker face. It hadn't been overly expressive to begin with. "I've been in the aviation industry all my life; my father flew a Harrier in the Gulf War and ran an air taxi service to Mackinac Island. I soloed at sixteen. I was a tomboy, Inspector: soapbox races, sharpshooting contests, first girl in my county to play Pee-Wee Football. If I'd started committing the book of regs to memory back then, I might just finish before I drew Social Security—if it's still around then. I let the desk pilots in Washington work out questions of jurisdiction." A shoulder twitched. "They'll want to ask me some things, so we'll be going over them together, first pass. I can tell you what shows; if they don't slap a gag on me."

"In that case, and if it's homicide, they'll hear from the city attorney. *We* got dibs on that."

"Is that all, Inspector? I have people to answer to who will be only too happy to hang this around my neck. Keeping them waiting won't help my chances."

"For now." He traded his folder for his cell and gave her a card. "That's mine. What's yours?"

She rattled off a number, which he entered. I did, too; but when Alderdyce saw me tapping keys I turned away and pretended I was having that conversation with my client. When I turned back, he was shaking Palm Volker's hand again. She strapped on her helmet, mounted up, and kicked the vintage motor back into life. I waited until she'd blatted off, then slid my phone back into my pocket. "Couldn't get through."

"Keep trying. Pretend you're a telemarketer." Alderdyce tapped my chest with his cell. "I'll check up on Strickling. Keep your phone on meanwhile, because you're going to connect the dots when I call back. The chief will want a person of interest to feed to the coyotes, at least until the next news cycle. If you don't give us something better they can chew on you."

The ambulance came just then, no lights or sirens to bother our sorry old planet about, an unmarked SUV from the medical examiner's office on its rear bumper. It gave Alderdyce an excuse to leave me with his curtain line, so I let him have it. I needed all the points I could rack up.

Anyway it was a break I could use. I slid around a barricade and headed toward the office on blocks, where Palm Volker had parked her Indian before going inside.

NINE

The place hadn't been entirely converted to an office. A two-burner stove, white enamel sink, and freckled Formica countertops shared space with an easy-assemble desk and two gray file cabinets in what had been the dining nook. A paper chart tacked to one wall illustrated a variety of planes in silhouette, like in the headquarters of an RAF squadron in a war movie, and framed prints, mostly of vintage airships, hung at careless angles on the birch paneling. Six feet of varnished wood propeller decorated the back wall near the ceiling, a little off level, like a bow tie skewed on purpose. Somebody was trying to tell me something; or someone if not me.

Biker Chick had been replaced by a businesswoman, calmly pleading her case from a dorm-room swivel to a buzzing male voice on the other end of the phone. She'd shed the leathers and wore a pale blue silk blouse with a spread collar that showed off the tan pillar of her neck. She was a curious blend of femininity and brute strength; then again, that was a lot to get from just a neck.

Liquid amber eyes flicked my way, then back to whatever she was scribbling on a yellow legal pad. It was a doodle of frightful faces hanging from the branches of a family tree like ugly fruit.

In my work you develop a talent for identifying words and images upside-down.

"Not the kind of clan you want to marry into," I said, when she'd hung up.

She glanced down at the sheet. "I did; but you can quit a marriage, just like you can quit a job. That gargoyle in Armani didn't introduce us," she added.

"It's a knockoff. John's one of the honest ones. He just has a good cutter." I selected a card without dog ears and smoothed it out on her pad. She read it where it was, folded her hands on the desk, and opened her face. It would be boyish after a haircut, except for the eyelashes. She was fast becoming my favorite person on this one; not that the bar was all that high. I drew up a plastic deck chair and sat. "I'm the eyewitness."

"Friend of yours?"

"Passing acquaintance. We didn't quite bond. What do you know about Golden Eagle Excursions?"

"They're paid up through the end of the year."

"Call them yet?"

"Line's busy. I called my senior to report."

"I take it you're still employed."

"What is it you want, Mr. Walker?"

"Clare Strickling, that's the dead man, beat a path to that hangar from an interview with me at his place in Saline. He's suspected of profiting from an illegal stock trade. When someone with a hot bundle visits an airfield, the long arm of coincidence drags clear to the ground. What I want to know is if Golden Eagle has a history of carrying passengers without, let's say, filing a flight plan."

She tipped her head of chestnut curls toward a window with louvered panes. It looked out on private hangars, a red-and-white storage shed pretending to be a small barn, and a mesh cone hanging from a pole, stirring idly in the slight breeze. "You see that windsock? There are high-tech devices that can measure wind direction and velocity to within a thousandth of a degree, but this field makes do with the same technology used by the Wright brothers. It's all my boss can afford. So when a customer pays his rent square on time we don't ask him if he's smuggling in Lithuanian terrorists or heroin from Amsterdam or exporting guns to insurrectionists in the Republic of Who Gives a Rat's Ass. He might take offense, demand his money back, and post an uncomplimentary review on our web site."

"So that's a no comment."

Just then a squat aluminum pot with an S-shaped spout squealed on the stove. She got up, slid it to an inactive burner, and took cups and saucers from a cupboard above the sink. "I don't suppose you drink tea."

"If you put a nail in it, sure."

She poured boiling water into the cups, dandled a bag in each, and let them steep while she fetched a bottle of Ten High from another cupboard. She sweetened each cup and brought them to the desk, setting one in front of me.

"That was my dad's brand," I said, breathing in the steam. "He used to make deliveries to old Dodge Main. Second-generation bootleggers brought the stuff to the parking lot in the trunks of their cars. He said it traveled better than the premium labels."

"Let me guess. Driving a truck was good enough for the old man, but you set your sights higher."

"Not much, but it's easier on the back." I lifted my cup. She sipped from hers without returning the toast. Setting it down, she dragged over her pad, laid a steel straightedge across the middle of the page below the doodles, and wrote on the bottom half; right-handed, but with a left-handed slant. I once knew what that said about a person, but I couldn't remember it. I was more interested in her other movements. She tore off the lower portion and handed it to me. I stored away the fruits of all this observation in my virtual desk drawer, among the pins, ticket stubs, and Bazooka

Joe comic strips that cluttered it. Sometimes they turn into something.

I looked at the name and address she'd written. "Jack Flagg. Sounds like an emcee in a burlesque house."

"Close. He's a retired barnstormer, or so he says. I met him two or three times when he took out the lease on that hangar. Apart from that I've only seen the name on his checks, and they clear. His pilots keep changing, but their ID tags match the register, which he updates each month." She gestured with her teacup toward a bullet-shaped computer monitor on the corner of the desk. "Pre-arranged code. No, I don't know what kind of merchandise Golden Eagle flies or who or where to. Private air services aren't required to file flight plans or register their customers. It's still a free country—in parts, anyway."

The address was an office in the Healy Building downtown; not as impressive as it sounds. Landlords had been offering prospective tenants sweetheart rental arrangements with easy escape clauses since before the city went bankrupt. I thanked her, folded the sheet, and sat back with my tea-and–Ten High. "How much do you know about that model of plane?"

"What's *not* to know? One private puddle-jumper is pretty much like all the rest when they leave the factory. Some are faster, some have a higher ceiling, some handle like silk on glass, others like a junk wagon on a washboard road. Piper's a good ship. That's why you can't throw a fit on any airfield in this country without hitting one."

"What I'm hearing is it's a dull and dependable old milk horse."

"I'm no snob. If I were stuck on a desert island with no more room to take off than a batting cage, there isn't another bird I'd hope was coming to my rescue."

"It's just not sexy."

She ignored that. "For my money the finest aircraft ever made was the Sopwith Snipe. It practically flew itself, sometimes literally; during World War One it was known to land with a dead man at the stick." She leaned that demonstrative head toward one of the pictures on the wall, a period black-and-white shot of a Great War biplane perched on a muddy field. It looked like a box kite, fragile and graceful and eager to kick gravity with the first friendly breeze.

I grinned. "That's the one Snoopy flies."

"That was the Camel; also a good ship, but no Snipe. That bus out there inside the barricades isn't a patch on either of them."

"Could anyone rig it to taxi along the ground at a good enough clip to run down a man and chop up his head with the propeller, no one at the wheel, or would that require a pilot with experience?"

"Such as me."

"I'm not suspecting you. Should I?"

She took a nip and clicked the cup back into its saucer. "You phrase that like a detective, but you sound like you're asking me if I have any hobbies. Is this a first date?" She tapped the rim with a nail. It rang like a chime.

"I'm too old for you, Ms. Volker. I'm trying to get a line on just how many people *couldn't* have killed Clare Strickling."

"You're S.O.L. then, Mr. Walker. It's just like a car: Turn the key, jam a stick or something against the wheel, monkey with the throttle, slip the brake, and kick out the chocks. When the police finish checking out that hot rod, that's likely what they'll find. Any kid who figured out how to poke a playing card between the spokes of his Schwinn to make it sound like a Harley could do it."

I made some doodles of my own on the back of the folded sheet from the yellow pad, as if I were taking notes on the various types of aircraft and how they could be turned into a weapon. An oval face with long lashes and a square chin took shape under a leather aviator's helmet. I was wrong. It wasn't boyish even then. "How's chances of getting a look at those surveillance videos before the cops snap them up?"

"In return for what?" She too was sitting back, holding her cup between both hands as if to warm them. "Don't be taken in by the kind of front we put up. We're not a benevolent organization."

"I got that much from how you treat your office supplies. Any business that carves the budget that close to the bone doesn't sling around fat Christmas bonuses."

"Don't be taken in by it that way either. Everything's going into the expansion. If you're offering me a bribe it better be enough to make it worth going back to flying puddle-jumpers for Trans-Third-World Airlines."

"Something tells me you wouldn't do it even then. I'm asking a favor, not conspiring to commit a felony. I can wait while you make the arrangements; that just puts me on the scene when you get your hands on the video. Alderdyce didn't say you couldn't show material that belongs to the people you work for to a curious party."

"And what would make me so generous?"

I slid the sheet into an inside breast pocket. "Well, now that we've eliminated the legal risks, let's talk about that Christmas bonus."

She swirled the stuff in her cup. "You're not so old, Mr. Walker. The best plane I ever flew had ten thousand hours on its engine, and it was just getting broken in."

TEN

She picked up the phone and dialed a number. The conversation, at least on her end, was in Spanish; not, I could tell, pure Castilian by any stretch, but convincingly fluent. Although I couldn't follow it, it shaped up to go on for a while. She seemed to be trying to make herself understood and it took patience. I held up my cell, got a nod, and stepped outside to call my client, for real this time.

He wasn't answering his cell and when I called his office and hacked my way through the underbrush to someone who called herself his administrative assistant, she said he was on a plane headed for Texas and couldn't be reached.

Palm was still straddling the language barrier when I went back in, so I strolled the narrow office looking at pictures. One I'd thought was vintage wasn't; it just looked antique because it was in black-and-white and the plane was an open-cockpit job that looked like one of the ones King Kong had swatted at on top of the Empire State Building. The pilot standing next to it was Palm Volker, in boots and cords. A pair of goggles dangled from her hand on a hip. They'd left a clean white mask around her eyes from the smoke or oil spray that smudged the rest of her face. Her rectangular jaw and solemn expression resembled Amelia Earhart's in every photo of her I'd ever seen.

Just about the time I identified her, the phone conversation ended. She stood the receiver in its niche and said, "The police wouldn't let my guy past the barricade, but he's on his way with the video from the hangar next door. That one's unassigned. I can't guarantee the quality; no sense spending an extra buck on a place that's not paying rent. I doubt the inspector will be interested. Angle it's at, whoever shows up probably can't be tied definitely to the scene of the crime—'scene of the crime,' my God!—but then you're not interested in pleading the case in court, are you?"

I didn't answer. I tapped the glass in the picture frame. "When you were bragging up the virtues of the Sopwith Snipe, I didn't realize it was from personal experience."

She got up to come over and stand beside me. "Not quite. That's a Gypsy Moth. It was supposed to be an anniversary gift, but the marriage fell through before the deal. At least I got to take it for a test ride."

I didn't know if two divorce references were intended to invite an other-than-professional suggestion on my part. I didn't have time to tinker with it.

"You shouldn't have told me that," I said, "about the cops not caring what's on that particular tape. With evidence-tampering off the table I might not be so inclined to test your integrity."

"There's Càndido. We can haggle when he's gone."

A heavy foot had struck one of the two-by-sixes that made up the steps to the door. It opened without a knock and a stocky gaucho in greasy coveralls with a mane of tangled hair to his shoulders came in carrying a plastic jewel case. He had the broad face and earnest eyebrows of Emiliano Zapata. The eyes slid past me without registration, a few words were exchanged in that same bastard dialect of the phone call, and then Palm and I were left alone with the video and a lingering essence of motor oil, stale sweat, and Old Milwaukee. The pagan idol inked on the laborer's left wrist had been made with a jackknife and a crushed Bic pen;

but it's none of my business when an employer takes a chance on an ex-convict. They make up enough of the local workforce to form their own union.

"How many languages do you speak?" I said.

Palm opened the case and started wrestling with the metallic disc stuck inside. "Just three, if you count my high-school English and cut me some slack on Spanish and just enough French to get me into trouble. I flew a mail plane for six months in Zacatecas and ran a tourist service in Quebec for almost three years; I was a playing-manager there, shuttling fishermen from Montreal to Newfoundland and on one occasion a team of treasure hunters to Baffin Island, looking for Viking gold. There!" The disc popped loose with a noise like a pistol shot. "Càndido's not a fan of strangers, you might have noticed."

"Maybe he's just shy. How does one get from Baffin Island to Detroit?"

"Guess."

"The ex-husband."

"We were in business together there. We owned a two-seater Beechcraft and a half-interest in the Gypsy Moth. I'm an aviation history geek; when we got to the bargaining table I swapped him the Beechcraft for our part of the Moth. I had to sell that to the partner when Ottawa wouldn't renew my work visa. The market in private pilot jobs was soft at the time. Still is; and that's the whole tragic story, edited for content and formatted to fit your screen. This is crap."

She was holding the disc up to the light, studying the unlabeled side. It looked scraped and smutty.

"You can get stacks of blanks at Staples for next to nothing," she said, "but the skinflints in accounting want me to wipe and re-record the old ones until they don't even make good coasters. Cross your fingers and hope for nothing." She stooped to insert the DVD in the computer tower lodged in the kneehole of the desk.

The CRT monitor was mounted on a swivel. She turned it our way, bent over the desk, and beat a tympani on the keyboard. A pop-art tribute to Smilin' Jack vanished from the screen, followed by static lines, then a time stamp with that day's date. She clucked her tongue at the hour on display; it was pre-dawn: The field's tower lights didn't penetrate that far into the dark, and infrared was no more in the budget than fresh discs. She clicked more keys. A squirmy line and the rapid-changing numbers on the digital clock said fast-forward was in play.

Finally we got a look at a pair of oblongs that resembled airplane hangars, set corner-to-corner to each other. She slowed things down. The camera was focused on the building in the foreground—clearly it belonged to that one—with what might have been the back end of Golden Eagle just visible at an oblique angle. Not the whole thing, but what we saw included most of the door I'd seen open at the back of the hangar. It was closed, with the overhang of the roof concealing one corner.

"Camera's mounted too high," Palm muttered. "Maybe we'll catch a break. Could be our killer shaves his head and has his name and Social Security number tattooed on his scalp."

I said nothing. We were still several hours away from Strickling's and my arrival on the scene. She revved up the action, hands hovering over the keys now, stopping and backing up from time to time for a closer look when something or someone moved into sight. A coveralled maintenance worker in a pith helmet pawed unambitiously at some loose asphalt with a leaf rake and went away leaving the job half-done; a seagull foraging new territory beyond the river swooped at what might have been a lump of chewing gum on the pavement and then away with an indignant thumping of wings. A Styrofoam cup bounced across the ground; ten seconds of entertainment in the middle of a long stretch of nothing. The Suburban beater I'd seen earlier cruised between the buildings and out of sight. A moment later, the surly Càndido got my heart beating when he strode in the opposite direction through the triangle of space and paused, looking left and right, but he went on out of the frame and didn't come back. I was disappointed, with him and myself; it was my prejudice showing. It was no business of mine what a man carved into his own arm.

We were close now, if the timer was anywhere near accurate. I leaned in as if I were looking to catch myself on camera; but I'd never been closer than forty feet to that part of the field, and anyway I'm not all that eager to see myself as others do.

We raised something at last. A broad black back strode in from the lower right corner; strode with the casual elaborateness of an experienced actor crossing a stage, half-aware of an audience, but ignoring it as something of no consequence. The head turned slightly right and left, but the overhead angle was too steep to make out the face even in profile. The body that belonged to the head didn't hesitate. It got to Golden Eagle's back door, tried the knob, bent over it, and went to work, its hands hidden by its body. This went on for a while. The key didn't seem to be cooperating; if it was a key.

I looked again at the clock. This was minutes before Strickling came to the other end of the building. The timing couldn't be worse for a routine break-in.

The time stamp seemed to slow then, crawling through the digits. It didn't, of course; but by then we were watching a pot that was stubbornly determined not to come to a boil.

Right in the middle the image in front of us froze. We might not have noticed, because there was nothing animate on the screen; but the numbers stopped changing. Palm punched a key, with no result. Time stood still another few seconds; then the screen went blue.

"Damn!" She smacked the desk with the heel of her hand. "Too scratched up! The nickel-squeezing sons of bitches!"

I wanted to calm her down, but it wasn't my secret to share.

A trained fighter always enters the ring left shoulder foremost. It doesn't matter how long it's been since he laced on a pair of gloves last; it's wired in by years of experience. I'd seen it myself recently. I'd have known who the man on camera was, even if he'd worn a bag over his head.

I'd been premature in my earlier assessment. There was exactly as much to Gabe Parrish as met the eye.

ELEVEN

She tried a few more times to advance the disc, but it froze up in the same spot every time. She gave up, popped it out, and returned it to its case. She held it in front of her in both hands like a shield.

"This isn't proof of anything. I don't know if I should even bother to show it to the police *or* the FAA."

"Better show it to both. The cameras the cops are guarding inside the barricades will be even less help. Our killer didn't come that direction. Fuzzy as he is, that character we were just looking at is the one who sent that plane after Strickling."

"I can't see it," she said. "Take someone's life over a shady stock deal? You wouldn't believe the crap you have to do just to operate a legitimate service some places—the only difference between Montreal and Mexico is the exchange rate with the crooked U.S. dollar—but I'm still naïve when it comes to this kind of thing. Unless you're not giving me the full story." Her eyes went from honey to ice.

"Of course I'm not. I'm running a legitimate service myself." I looked at my watch. I wondered if Yale had landed in Texas. If he returned my call I needed to be alone. I asked her if there was somewhere I could get in touch with her after hours.

She hesitated. "I can't think of any information I could provide beyond what I have."

"Neither can I. It doesn't mean I won't later." I gave her fifty dollars in Dowling case cash from my wallet. She looked down at the creased bill.

"I'm not so cheap a date as that."

"This isn't flirting. I promised you a bonus."

She stretched out the fifty, frowning at it, then poked it down her front. She put her left-handed slant to the pad and handed me the sheet. She lived on East McNichols. That was convenient; she wouldn't burn a pint of gas commuting to work on her bike.

"A whole sheet." I folded it. "Are we flirting now?"

"No."

She sat down and dialed, waited, said, "Accident Investigation, please. I have a fatality to report."

You live, you learn, you die dumb. If you have to ask, the answer is always no.

Back behind the wheel I thought again of Yale, but let my phone be. A pair of city uniforms stood in front of the sawhorses around the plane plowed nose-down into the berm near the fence. One of them was smoking, the other killing time on his cell. Both looked my way, for no other reason than I was something to distract them from the least entertaining part of the job. I didn't know if the cop with the phone could pick up random calls on some kind of scanning app; I hadn't been one of them for a generation. It's getting so you can't make an honest buck the dishonest way without running into technology.

The green portfolio lay on the passenger's seat, the folder that Clare Strickling had been guarding so closely until he lost his head. I made it a point not to look at it or think about it, once I remembered it was there. Reading minds is a police trick older than IBM.

I took the direct route downtown by way of Gratiot. That benevolent jack-o'-lantern shade of sunshine had turned to bright brass: In our zone you can get all four seasons on one plate. The traffic lulled and the city turned on all the green lights for me. By the time I figured I was far enough out of surveillance range to use the cell, I was so close to the office I might as well call from my landline. I was pulling into my personal space in front of the latest vacancy in the jinxed retail building across from mine when the cell rang. It was my client.

"My assistant said you were trying to reach me. Did you find out anything?"

"Where are you?"

"In the back of a town car, crawling down I-45. The entire Galveston plant's threatening to walk out and the union brass won't negotiate with anyone else but me. My takeoff was delayed; I've got just an hour to make the meeting, so tell me this is a pleasant diversion. What have you found out?"

"More about aviation than I ever wanted to know. Is Gabe Parrish with you?"

"No. He doesn't fly, and anyway he's got too much to do back home without wet-nursing his boss on a last-minute business trip. Why are you calling me if you don't have anything to report? And what's this about aviation? No, forget that. What's so important about Parrish you need to know where he is?"

"Later." I boiled down the developments for him, minus what I'd seen on the video; that needed ripening. He listened without interrupting, then: "My God."

"You asked what I found out. I never said I didn't have anything to report."

"Think Weatherall killed Strickling?"

"He's on an electronic tether. Even if he slipped it, this deal suggests planning. If you're right and Strickling wound Weath-erall up and set him loose on your stepson, someone else had to have set this one up. It isn't the kind of brainwork you expect from a freeway shooter." I didn't want to steer the conversation back to Parrish; it would be too easy for Yale's security chief to get wind of it. I was one up on him until he did.

"I see what you mean," Yale said. "Think Strickling was leav-ing the country?"

"Not just yet. He was expecting someone when I dropped in on him. The longer I hung around the more nervous he got. Finally he made a call, probably shifting the appointment to the airfield. At a guess he was making travel arrangements for later, but someone had other ideas." The portfolio on the passenger's seat stuck in the corner of my eye. That's where it had to stay until I knew for sure what was in it; not that I couldn't guess. "It's a police matter now, so I'm going to have to give them something. What about it?"

"Can't you hold them off?"

"Not if I don't throw them a bone. If there isn't as much meat on it as they think there should be, they'll tank me for obstruction of justice or as a material witness. It won't hold, and they won't expect it to. It's just leverage to make me crack. I'm no good to you in the cage, so I might as well give them something before I have to wait out the paperwork."

A semi or something passed his ride, walloping it with slip-stream. He waited it out.

"Okay," he said then. "Tell them what I hired you for. I'll rely on your judgment as to how much detail you think they can handle."

"Thanks. I'll fill in the blanks later." I thumbed off.

Gabe didn't fly. That was rich, for some reason.

Someone was whistling on the first landing on the way up to my office. The tune came with sabers and squatting Cossacks. Knowing our building superintendent, he'd switched from "Oklahoma" when he heard someone coming. Rosecranz got his accent from Boris Badenov and ordered his caviar from Salt Lake City. He was standing on top of a wooden stepladder stained all over with white paint, swishing dead bugs around inside the globe he'd removed from the ceiling fixture.

I looked at the date on my watch. "Chinese New Year already?"

A face like an old boot looked down at me. "You are so funny I am almost forgetting to laugh."

"Close," I said. "Next time try rolling the *r*'s."

He said something he'd memorized from the bill of fare at the Little Slice of Minsk and dumped the exoskeletons out onto the linoleum. I stepped around them and the ladder and climbed the rest of the way to my floor.

The landline rang as I was unlocking the door to the parsonage. I crossed the square of carpet remnant in two strides and leaned across the desk to pick up.

"Amos Walker?"

I admitted as much.

"This is Leonora Feeney."

I tried to place the name, also the voice, which kept going up and down the scale. It sounded like a loose fan belt.

She helped me out. "Judge Kitchner's personal assistant. I have that information you asked for. About Melvin Weatherall?"

If Yale hadn't asked about him on the phone, I might not have recognized that name either, right away. He was just the man who'd killed Lloyd Lipton and landed me a client. It didn't seem possible I'd been asking about him in Gale Kitchner's chambers only that same day.

I took down the information and thanked her; but Weatherall could wait. He was on a tether after all. I broke the connection, fished out my notebook, and called Jack Flagg at Golden Eagle Excursions before I could rack up any more murders.

"Flagg here."

I grinned at the wall opposite the desk. He had the bluff, hearty voice of a carnival barker. When a character runs true to type, everything in the universe falls into order. I told him who I was and what I did for a living.

"More detectives?" Chewing gum cracked on his end. "I'll save us both the rest of the morning: I didn't know any Clare Strickling; there wasn't nobody on duty at the hangar this week, business is shit; and when the hell can I get one of my best planes out of hock with the cops so I can check out the damage to tell my insurance company? 'Cause if a flock of sparrows can twist a prop like a corkscrew and fuck up ten thousand bucks' worth of engine, what do you think a human skull would do?"

There was more in that strain. I only half-listened, propping the receiver between my chin and my shoulder, while I unzipped the green portfolio and removed the package from inside.

When he paused—probably to spit out his gum—I took advantage of the interruption to say I'd get back to him when he wasn't so busy. Then I hung up and unwound the bricks of currency from their blue wrapping.

TWELVE

The cloth was Velcro, which made an ugly noise when I tore it open. I counted the bills; I was getting to be good at that for someone who kept a charge account at Dollar General. They were crisp, all uncirculated hundreds and fifties, except for a packet of twenties. It came to an even twenty thousand. I made room for it in the safe among the odd papers, the small green strongbox that held petty cash, and a bottle of Old Smuggler, the bootleggers' friend, closed the door and spun the dial. That would slow down a correspondence-school cracksman for a couple of minutes.

It was evidence; or it was until I could figure out what to do with it, endow a kennel at the Humane Society or buy a match girl her own pushcart. A lot of money would only confuse my banker.

Next I turned my attention to the portfolio. It was a quality item made of stiff twill, with the Yale logo intalgioed in a brown leather-type patch on the outside. The left-hand slant of the letters made me think of Palm Volker's penmanship; that wasn't pertinent to the investigation, and I wondered why she should have come to mind. Brown leather piping inside and a clear plastic pocket, framed in brown leather also, designed to hold a business card in case the portfolio was misplaced and some honest person cared to return it to its owner. The card inside was blank except for the company name. I left it where it was.

Everything was clean and bright-smelling, like a new phonograph record. Assuming it had come zipped from the manufacturer, I might have been only the second person to open it. A trio of file pockets was built in for storing documents. What they contained didn't look like any business of Yale's: travel brochures, unfolding to show glossy photos of teal-colored water, white sands, bikinis, champagne flutes, and roulette wheels; happy handsome people having the time of their lives in resorts with names I couldn't pronounce. It was a tour of the world's pleasure spots, none of which resembled Michigan.

Strickling wouldn't have been going to any of those places. It was a blind, to be left with whoever the money was intended for. At least that's what I thought; you don't find this level of skullduggery in the bleacher section.

I turned the portfolio toward the light and spread the folders, looking for a nugget of intel stuck in a seam. A scrap of white made my heart jump, but it was just a label stitched in by a sweatshop worker in China.

Twenty grand was a steep price to pay for airfare, without so much as an in-flight movie or a packet of pretzels to pass the weary hours. Strickling had to have hit the jackpot on the stock exchange to make it worthwhile. I wondered what he'd done with the rest, although it was pretty certain some kind of electronic transfer was involved. As chiselers went he was no credit union drone with a ticked-off wife in Royal Oak. I couldn't expect to stumble over *two* overcoats stuffed with folding the same week.

It was quite a three-pipe problem.

Not being a pipe smoker I burned three cigarettes in succession, then dragged over the phone and dialed the number Mrs. Feeney had just given me. There was small danger of flushing this one into flight with a call. A court-ordered electronic tether alerts the authorities to an escape attempt the minute it crosses a line three blocks from the defendant's front door. A trained sleuth like Walker could canvass an area that size without breaking a sweat.

"Hello."

He was used to answering the phone a lot; the lack of a question mark at the end suggested that. Someone, a lawyer or a nervous bail bondsman or some crank who made a practice of calling felons whose names had appeared in the news to pass judgment on his ancestry, would keep his bell ringing, and a man in his position couldn't afford to ignore it in case it was the governor calling with a pardon.

"Mr. Weatherall?"

"Who's calling?"

A shallow voice; it would die short of any stool pigeons listening next door. He'd know his way around an eight-by-ten cell.

I told him my name. "I'm a detective assigned to investigate the shooting on I-75 last month."

He was quicker on the uptake than I'd expected. "Assigned by who? Are you a cop?"

"I'm private, acting on behalf of an interested party. I don't have the authority to take you into custody. Anything you tell me will be entirely voluntary. It might even help your case."

That was laying it on with a shovel. I made a symbol on the desk pad in my personal shorthand to remind me not to jump to unprofessional conclusions concerning the other party's intelligence. It was shaped like a dunce cap: seven and a half, my size.

Ambient air stirred on his end, flavored slightly by a deep heavy remote thumping. His neighbors either had a superior stereo system or they were breaking through a wall. There would be a lot of that kind of thing in the kind of place he would live. A mental coin was being flipped.

"What the hell," he said then. "I'm bored out of my skin hanging around this dump all day. Bring a couple of forties and we'll have us a party."

"No drinking restrictions on your release?"

"Can I help it if somebody bootlegs it in?"

I said I'd be dropping by.

"Anytime, dude. You'll find me home." He cackled.

I listened to the dial tone, then put the receiver back on its hook. I was thinking of breaking the bottle out of the safe, using the cash as an excuse—just to make sure a mouse hadn't run off with it—when the old building shook under the punishment of a pair of hand-lasted gunboats on the stairs. I knew that tread; knew also that when the man who owned it wanted to, he could take two flimsy flights as quietly as smoke rising. I waited until a board bent in the hall outside, then called out to John Alderdyce to come ahead in.

He had on the same gray suit, but had changed into a powder-blue shirt with a starched white collar and a necktie whose horizontal red-and-black stripes did nothing to reduce his bulk. He mowed his hair so close to the scalp it looked like gray moss on glazed obsidian and showed all the dents and declivities in his long skull. Some he'd been born with; the rest came from using his head for a battering ram. There wasn't a door in the city's war zone he hadn't been first through.

I said, "What'd you do, annex Lord and Taylor to the Second Precinct?"

He fingered his half-Windsor. "You know me. Fresh threads are like a good stiff belt after ten minutes with a festering boil like you." He grasped the stiff wooden chair facing the desk as if to pull it out, then remembered it wouldn't budge and sat in it as it was. "Bolted down like always. Still got a piece rigged under the desk in line with your visitors' bellies?"

"I'm traveling in more genteel circles these days. And I've got only the one gun."

"Only the one we've got paperwork on, you mean. Talk to your client?"

"His name's Emmett Yale. You probably know the name; he's Elon Musk out of Henry Ford. He had a stepson named Lloyd Lipton who drove his cherry Stingray into the path of a bullet up near the zoo the day of the Dream Cruise, fired by a bottom-feeder named Melvin Weatherall. Yale thinks Clare Strickling put Weatherall up to it because Lipton sold him some illegal stock information. He was the only one who could connect Strickling to a federal offense."

"Any evidence Lipton did that?"

"That's the job. Heat like that would explain why Strickling went to Palm Volker's airfield, looking for safe passage out of U.S. jurisdiction, and maybe why he never left; but that part's your headache, not mine."

"What tipped you off he was blowing the country?"

Determinedly I didn't think about what was in the safe or the folder in the desk drawer.

"I don't know that he was. He could've been an airplane buff. Some people get a buzz out of watching them take off and land." I opened a palm. "Okay. So long as I don't have to repeat it on video downtown, because it's all just gut."

"Why do you think I came slumming around here instead of having you frog-walked into the Second?"

I told him what I'd told Yale over the phone, about spooking Strickling into changing his appointment and then tailing him to the airfield.

"I gave you the rest," I said. "It looks more and more like Yale's hunch is right. If someone thought Strickling was worth taking out, it stands to reason Lipton was too; domino effect. Whoever that someone is, if Strickling himself is innocent of murder, he's getting more sophisticated. He went from a run-of-the-mill free-way shooting to vehicular homicide involving a plane."

"You may be oversimplifying things, rolling two murders into one just for the convenience."

"Could be. Maybe Strickling set the tone and this one's just got more imagination."

I left out what I'd seen on the disc at the airfield. He'd know almost as much as I did when Palm played it for him, and in any case it didn't prove Parrish had done anything, or for that matter if it *was* Parrish; you don't have to be an ex-pug to walk like one. Right now, Gabe Parrish was my fallback guy if and when my other leads petered out, which they do at some point almost every time.

Nevertheless, it seemed this time I was leaving out a lot more than usual. I needed a pocket reminder to help me keep track of it all.

"Imagination." He grinned; not his most reassuring expression. "The working homicide cop's best friend. Sooner or later these idea boys get too razzle-dazzle for their own good."

"So who gets to sweat Weatherall, me or Detroit's Finest?"

He pushed himself to his feet. It wasn't until he stood up you remembered how big a chunk of the universe he claimed as his own. The ceiling was high by this century's standards, but you cringed, waiting for his head to bust through the plaster. On the other hand, he could make himself seem smaller just by sitting down and hunching his shoulders; he grew or shrank to suit the situation, like something from Lewis Carroll.

"You take Melvin," he said. "I mix with that swill every day, now it's your turn. You can add what you find out to your eyewitness statement; which unlike the IRS we don't grant extensions on, keep that in mind. Right now I'm headed back to City Airport, watch the people come and go on video."

I wanted to tell him not to hold out much hope. Instead I said: "Easy to look at, isn't she?"

He shook his head. "I'm too married, and you're too old. We got to treat the Palm Volkers of this world like bank tellers count cash; pretend it's Monopoly money."

He made no noise at all going back downstairs.

THIRTEEN

Melvin Weatherall lived in Ferndale, in an affordable-housing development built near the old state fairgrounds off Woodward. On the way I passed a barbecue stand next door to a discount hubcap store; the residual aroma of roasting fat and sticky-sweet sauce coming through my window reminded me I hadn't eaten much breakfast. I made a U-turn and parked next to a fireplug.

The place was called Uncle Zeke's Gospel 'n' Gobble and had a sandwich-board sign on the sidewalk reading THE END IS NEAR; meaning the stand was scheduled to close for the season come the first of November. The structure was a box of slapped-together plywood with a primitive Jesus painted on the front, blessing the place holding two pork ribs in the shape of a cross; I couldn't decide if it was blasphemy or piety. At the window I bought half a rack wrapped in greasy newspaper, coleslaw in a plastic cup, and a beaded bottle of Purple Gang beer, and ate sitting at a picnic table where I could watch the car and keep an eye out for cops.

The gnome at the counter—who wasn't a licensed package-liquor dealer, not by half—sold me a six-pack of Purple Gang, charging a premium price that included the paper sack he put it in, with CHENE-FERRY MARKET block-printed on the outside, a re-cycled item. That advertising might give me plausible deniability when I showed up on a surveillance camera delivering it to a defendant out on bail.

At the apartments, some attempt had been made to supply dignity to the impoverished with a bas-relief frieze of colonial columns along the sprawling front of the brick building and a faux-stone tablet sign with *Northland Manor* worked into it as if with a chisel; the Northland shopping center down the road had been demolished, so the name was up for grabs. Twenty years of auto-industry history shared slots in the parking lot, some of it on bald tires, one with a flat, and here and there a late-model Japanese convertible to break up the monotony; no low-end housing project is complete without a touch of welfare fraud. I was a snob about it and chose a spot between a patchwork of fenders and a sub-compact with opaque plastic taped over a broken window.

Weatherall's name was scrawled in colored pencil on a three-by-five card next to a numbered button in the airlock. It made a feeble attempt at a buzz when I pressed it, like a fly stuck in a web. It was a feeling I was familiar with.

A more virile answer sprang the lock on the inner door. I followed a narrow ground-floor hall to a slab of blank steel with just the number on a plastic strip in a slot next to it.

He might have been waiting for me on the other side, because it opened to the first rap of my knuckles. A gust of shut-up air and mildewed pizza boxes puffed out. It was all of a piece with the tenant. Weatherall looked even paler in person than he did at his arraignment, clay-colored, in fact: A completely bald head and a keyhole-shaped face only an Edvard Munch could love.

I thrust the paper sack into his arms. "When they ask, tell 'em I brought kielbasa."

He spread the top and looked inside. "Forties, I said."

"You don't have to drink them."

For answer he tucked the package under one arm and drew the

door open the rest of the way. A pair of eyes like wet kelp swept the hallway behind me before he shut it behind me.

The place was L-shaped, with the bathroom and sleeping quarters out of sight around the corner and the usual utilitarian arrangement of kitchenette, love seat and armchairs upholstered in stiff fabric, a floor lamp with a paper shade wrapped in plastic, and a green-and-orange rug in a swirly design like dishwater going down a drain. It wasn't exactly squalid, apart from the skunky odor of an inhabitant too long in residence, the old delivery containers attracting flies in the kitchenette, and a heap of Marlboro butts in a plastic saucer on a slick yellow wood table. Car and motorcycle magazines sprawled beside them, with the usual breast augmentations posing in bikinis on the covers. *Precious Moments–*type art hung on the walls, plus the modification of enormous mammaries to go with the big soulful eyes.

Two Asians in medieval armor hacked away at each other on a thirty-seven-inch TV with the sound turned off; closed-captioning chugged along with the dubbed-in dialogue on the bottom of the screen. A purple bong lay on the floor in front of a sliding glass door looking out on a phony balcony.

It was almost too spot-on, as if a set designer had been brought in to match the place to that species of creature whose remedy for boredom is taking target practice at motorists approaching an overpass.

The creature had on a dirty olive-drab tank top and khaki shorts with mustard stains on them. The bright orange band locked around his hairless right ankle was exposed, like some New Age accessory he was proud to show off. Low-cut sneakers exposed a pair of ankles that made his clothes look clean. He didn't smell as rank as a monkey house.

The beers were cold. He took out the six-pack, threw the sack in the general direction of a step-lid trash basket overflowing in the kitchenette, and opened two bottles by bracing the caps against the aluminum band binding a vinyl-topped counter and smacking them with the heel of his hand. The band was bent all over from previous procedures.

I didn't want a beer. I was still feeling bloated from the Gospel 'n' Gobble; but I took it when he handed it to me. An icebreaker is an icebreaker, no matter how low you got in society.

I sat next to him on the love seat, which gave not at all under my one-eighty, sipping from the bottle and watching him cruise through basic cable with a phallic remote: *Golden Girls,* cooking show, commercials, *Golden Girls,* CNN, *Golden Girls,* ESPN, a slew of music channels, an all-ethnic *Golden Girls* for the woke audience. The kung fu battle was still in progress every time we came back to it; neither combatant seemed to be making any headway. He was like a housefly that couldn't make up its mind where to light. He finished his first beer, got up, repeated the opening operation, and was back in his seat switching stations with barely an interruption.

This was how he would spend his days, whether alone or with company. I pretended it was meant to be a conversation starter, and asked him when was his sentencing date.

"November tenth." Swig, click.

"What's your lawyer say?"

"Five years; twenty-seven months, if I don't throw a hissy. If you can believe anything a P.D. says." Click, swig, belch.

"Not bad for a killing." I took a long pull. It tasted like the air in the apartment.

"It ain't so easy as all that. I got to squeeze out some tears in front of the judge."

"Why'd you do it, Melvin?"

He looked at me directly for the first time since he'd opened the door. His thumb stayed firm on the button. A lot of entertainment stuttered past on the screen without his notice. "Who'd you say you were?"

I told him. Took a shorter tug, swallowed, looking at him the whole time. "Lloyd Lipton's stepfather hired me to find out why he was killed."

That shook him so much he drained his second bottle in three gurgles. He might've done that if I were halfway across town, talking to someone else about some other case. You hear about psychopaths all the time, but you rarely see anyone who meets all the criteria. "I wasn't shooting at no Lloyds. I was shooting at a pretty blue-and-white sports job I'll never drive. I wasn't even aiming at him. It was payback for all the good luck he hogged from the rest of us."

There was a dent alongside his forehead that might have been made by a beer bottle swung by someone else on some other occasion. I wondered if mine would fit.

It was almost empty; I jiggled it significantly. He sprang up, like a good host, put two more dings in the counter rim, and returned to his seat, not exactly in a straight line. I figured a few days without a brew had made the stuff hit harder than usual. Five years in the coop could make him a teetotaler for what would surely prove to be a short life. He'd behave himself and get sprung in a little over two years—like I'd get to be governor.

I waited until he tipped his bottle up, then said, "I had a talk with Clare Strickling today."

He was supposed to choke and spew, but the beer slid the rest of the way down on greased runners.

He punched his chest and burped, "Who's that?"

"Maybe he didn't tell you his name. I don't suppose he wrote it on a check."

He leaned forward, releasing another blast of fermented hops, stood his beer on the some-assembly-required coffee table; it took two tries before he got it to stand upright. "Wha's deal?"

"You're too modest," I said. "Here you are posing as just another slug with a hard-on against the more evolved, when what you really are is a butcher for hire, a regular Machine Gun Mc-Gillicuddy. Too bad you come so cheap or you'd be drinking single malt in a condo in Grosse Pointe instead of slurping suds in a Ferndale dump."

I waited. It was like watching a poker chip sink into a stick of butter. Then he stirred. The remote control, abandoned, slid from his lap and thumped to the floor. His fingers had almost slipped off the bottle before he got a bright idea. I saw it take shape on his face, flickering to life like a faulty fluorescent tube. It was an interesting anthropological observation.

I let his hand slide up to fist the neck of the bottle, a slo-mo replay only in real time. When he turned slightly away to give it the momentum required I drove the heel of my free hand into that groove on his temple, hitting it with the same force he used to pop the cap off a bottle. He wasn't worth swinging mine and spilling beer on my suit.

It was all very peaceful. He slid into a pile in the corner of the love seat without even letting go of his beer. I took it from him gently and set it upright on the table; I'm neat like that. A mouth without a molar left in it dropped open and let out a noise like a diesel engine trying to start. I'd wasted energy; in another minute he'd have passed out on his own. I couldn't find it in me to regret the unnecessary exertion.

I'd overdone it. I couldn't tell if he'd taken offense at being called a proxy killer or a punk with an inferiority complex. But I'd just been looking for a second opinion. I knew which he was.

I left him snoring and tossed the place anyway.

It didn't tell me anything I hadn't known the second I laid eyes on the tenant. The bathroom wasn't any worse than you see in bus stations the big fleets don't stop at. I turned on the ventilator fan to keep my eyes from watering and checked out the prescription drugs made out to John Doe in the cabinet, riffled through the pornographic literature on a shelf next to the toilet, and took the

lid off the tank looking for some junk that might have been sup-
plied in lieu of cash by Weatherall's late benefactor, if he had one.
I was beginning to doubt it.

The bedroom wasn't much better on the senses, and just as
helpful as to anything stuffed under the foul mattress or taped to
the bottom side of drawers in the cardboard chest.

Nothing in the kitchenette except a freezer that had needed
defrosting a couple of leap years ago and some serious science
projects on the refrigerator shelves. I had to wipe my eyes again
when I swung the door shut.

Two things happened then.

Weatherall sucked in a bucket of air with a snort and someone
hit the buzzer in the foyer. I looked at the first, but he was just
resettling himself in a new position for sleep. I took one last look
around, in case he'd written his confession on a purloined letter
I'd overlooked, then let myself out.

Outside the door at the end of the hall I met a square-built
woman in a rose-colored suit with a knee-length skirt, thick-soled
shoes, and carroty hair in a buzz cut. She looked like the thickest
part of the Lions defensive line. She said she was with the district
court and was Melvin Weatherall in residence?

I jerked my thumb over my shoulder and held the door for her.
"Try not to trip on the beer bottles."

She stepped past me, her jaw set like a steam shovel.

FOURTEEN

It was slack time at the McDonald's on the corner of Seven Mile. I got coffee at the drive-thru without having to wait and parked in an unshaded spot to scorch my throat and clear the alcoholic fog from my cognitive centers. The air had taken a turn and the sun lay across the back of my neck like a warm towel.

Melvin Weatherall was your garden-variety lowlife. They breed in our town like rats; their choice of weapon is the blunt instrument, the flick knife, the anonymous handgun available in a parking lot near you. They don't hang out with the class of criminal that would chop a man's head into sweetmeats with a private plane. Even if they had access to one, they weren't capable of original thinking like that, or of the patience involved in targeting a single motorist with traffic at its peak. If Emmett Yale weren't so busy building cars and putting out labor fires and fencing with the National Transportation Safety Board and the half-dozen other federal agencies that oversee the auto industry, he'd have cleared Weatherall of premeditation in his stepson's death in less than a day, as I had. In fact, there was no reason for me to stay on the job he'd hired me for. I could turn over the cash in my safe and let the cops earn what I paid them in taxes.

Except if I walked away now I'd never sleep a night through without Clare Strickling's decapitated ghost sharing my bed.

Even now, every time I closed my eyes that crimson explosion of blood and brains splattered the inside of my lids.

The coffee was trying to climb back up my throat. I backed out of the space and stopped by the trash bin at the end of the driveway to dump the nearly full container.

D. J. Healy had run a dyeing operation around the time of the Cleaners and Dyers War of the 1920s, but had survived the protection racket to establish an empire in women's fashions. Six-and-a-half stories of Renaissance architecture north of the old Kern Block had sheltered the enterprise to mid-century, when other businesses muscled in, but its Edwardian character hangs on, like lavender in a grand old lady's lingerie drawer.

Two cops in uniform flanked a green SUV at the curb when I came around the corner from where I'd parked. They weren't taking chances now, even on a busted taillight.

A snap-letter directory in the marble lobby directed me to the fifth floor. The copper-plated elevator smelled like an old steamer trunk. The doors glided open on a hallway with a rubber-and-felt runner and bronze arrows indicating the numbers of office suites from five hundred on up.

GOLDEN EAGLE EXCURSIONS was lettered in gold on ridged glass in a door halfway down the hall. That same arrogant raptor stretched its wings underneath. I turned the low-slung brass knob and pushed open the door on a waiting room with no one to wait on me, just a pair of tweed-upholstered club chairs, a Lucite rack of travel brochures, and a burnt-orange rug. The walls were plastered with toothy señoritas, tanned skiers, and daredevils hanging from parachutes. That same bird scowled in the corner of each poster. SOAR WITH US, it demanded.

A hallway carpeted in the same cozy shade of sienna extended to the right and left of a square opening opposite the door. I wandered that direction and almost collided with a bell-shaped woman with gray hair clamped tight to her skull with glittering silver pins. An embroidered scarf swaddled her neck and one end hung to what used to be her waist. The purple dress she wore clashed with everything, like Peck's bad boy. Her glasses had more facets than a Fresnel lens. They gave her the eyes of a fly.

From instinct I threw out both my hands to her shoulders to keep her from falling over backward. She shook herself loose, also from instinct, and backed off three feet, clasping the sheaf of manila folders she was carrying to her bosom. "You don't have to be in such a hurry," she snapped. "We're here on a three-year lease."

She was the one who'd been in a hurry, but I apologized and opened my ID folder, snapping it shut before she got a good look at the badge. "I'm investigating the incident at your hangar. Have you heard from the police?"

Her mouth was working. She wasn't having a stroke; she was trying to read my lips. I repeated what I'd said, loud.

"You don't have to yell! Someone called from there. We're expecting them any time. I guess that's you. When can we have our insurance people look at the plane? We can't file a claim without an estimate of the damage."

I dialed it down a notch. "You'll have to talk to headquarters about that. I have sort of an appointment with Mr. Flagg. Is he available?"

"He's out to lunch."

I looked at my watch.

She said, "He has low blood sugar. You people can't expect him to wait all day for you without putting something in his stomach. Or maybe you do. You're so busy trying to find out why someone's dead you don't care whether someone else dies waiting to cooperate."

I apologized again. "Do you know when he'll be back?"

"No. You can do the waiting for a change." She jerked her glittering head toward the reception area.

"Yes, ma'am."

She made a noise in her throat and shot down the hall carrying her files.

I sat on one of the chairs, grabbed a brochure, and looked at cats swarming Hemingway's old house in Key West. After a minute I put it back and made another run into No Man's Land. It was as quiet as the Roman catacombs, but better lit, by way of copper canisters. There was one door down to the left and two to the right, the second at the very end of the hall. I went the way the woman had gone, eased open the first door. This room was a little bigger than a closet and contained only a credenza and a copying machine the size of a kitchen table. The credenza held a short stack of manila folders like the ones she'd been carrying. My guess was they were the same ones. I flipped open the top two: business correspondence, order forms, a fuzzy aerial shot of no place in particular. It left me no less ignorant than before. I let myself back out and tried the door at the end of the hall. It was blank steel and opened on a downward flight of metal-grid stairs and stale air, a fire exit. I wouldn't have thought the old bat scared that easy. I pulled the door shut and went the other direction, past the opening from the waiting area.

The ridged glass on the last door read PRIVATE. I rapped softly. A muffled voice on the other side invited me in.

This one was three times the size of the copying room, with a view of Cadillac Square through the rear window. More posters lined the walls, these unframed, some as large as queen beds, each featuring fragile-looking aircraft in flight, all at harrowing angles. One included the accessory of a blond stunner in tights balancing herself on a wing, blue sky and whipped-potato clouds in the background, gaudily painted by an artist apprenticed in the swashbuckling school. They were faded and torn, but you could read the red-and-yellow legend from across the street:

MAJOR JACK FLAGG'S FLYING CIRCUS
THRILLS!
CHILLS!
FEATURING
EDNA NORTH, WING-WALKING WIZARDESS OF THE WORLD!
AND
THE WORLD'S ONLY PLANE-TO-PLANE TRANSFER
ACCOMPLISHED IN MID-AIR!

Flashy as the décor was, I noticed it second.

The man seated behind the desk facing the door seemed to own only one suit: Either that or he got the friends-and-family discount at an undertakers shop. Gabe Parrish sat with one set of scarred knuckles resting on a gray steel semiautomatic pistol on the glass top, the muzzle facing me. He looked put out, as if I'd arrived early for an appointment I didn't know I had; then his face went smug.

"You heard the lady," he said. "He's out to lunch."

FIFTEEN

A director's-type chair of vinyl-and-bentwood construction faced the desk. I stepped around it, hands out from my sides, and sat. He had the drop on me anyway, and sometimes meekness is the best offense. I hoped this was one of those times.

I tested it. "He's not coming back from lunch, is he?"

It worked, or seemed to. He withdrew his hand from the pistol and settled back into the padded swivel behind the desk. "You got me all wrong. Right about now he's slurping truffle soup at the Blue Heron in Birmingham, on the Yale Mobility account; celebrating Golden Eagle's latest contract. He's to copter our security personnel to Metro airport when they're needed at any of our plants out of state."

"Not their chief, though. You don't fly, Yale says."

He gestured toward his head. "Inner ear, for which thanks. Many more shots to the melon and I'd've wound up taking drooling lessons. No, not me; and none of my people either. All the plants are fully staffed with personnel on-site."

"I thought no-show jobs were exclusive to the mob."

"The price wasn't steep when you consider the facts. Flagg's seventy-eight years old. He won't be around long enough to put us in the red."

"Where's the old lady?"

"Edna? Enjoying the fish course with her old man, Jack, if she didn't trip on the fire stairs and break her neck. That'd be ironic, huh? After all that derring-do." He jerked a thumb over his shoulder.

I looked at the vision waltzing on a wing in the poster. "I'll be damned. But you could've made the same kind of deal with Strickling and kept the Homicide squad out of it."

A muscle shifted in his face. His expression was hard to read because of all the dead battered skin. "See, that's why I went to all this trouble. I knew you'd figure out I was there when he got it and you'd be coming around here asking questions. If I wanted to kill him I'd've done it without flash. The idea would be to get it off the news as quick as possible. Use an airplane? Hell, it'd be a movie on HBO come Easter.

"Wasn't Flagg either," he went on. "I've been killing time here with his books. His profit margin is onionskin. You don't kill a fare without getting the money up front, and Strickling wouldn't part with it till he was buckled into his seat. He's not the only shark in the ocean."

"So what are you buying with this phony contract?"

"This." He swept a hand around the room. "The use of the office till quitting time, all for the price of a meal. It's worth that to keep your nose out of our corporate business. We got enough heat from Washington without a murder investigation. We'd be cleared, but the collateral damage in the meantime would put us into Chapter Eleven."

"How'd you know Strickling was planning to blow?"

"Don't be stupid. What else do you do when you made a sap out of a guy like Yale and stuck his wife's kid in the middle while you were at it? Not to mention killed—which I doubt he did. Weatherall? Please! You talked to him?"

I nodded. "That was a half-hour I won't get back."

"I could've saved you the trip. Anybody can see he couldn't

make up a shopping list, let alone plan a hit." He tilted the chair back on its swivel; that left the pistol as much within my reach as his. "No, that was just a bad break all around. That little prick Lipton wasn't worth it, Emmett knows that; but there's no accounting for a mother's love.

"I've had people on Strickling since he cashed in his 401(k) to scoop up that stock," he said. "His phone was tapped, so I knew where he was headed today before you did. Hell, I could've used what I knew about his deal with Flagg to set up this meeting we're having and save the dough; when you agree to fly a fugitive out of the country you're automatically an accomplice. A prosecutor could build a case on less."

"So why didn't you? Blackmail Flagg and save the dough?"

He rolled a shoulder.

"You never know how somebody will react to a squeeze, especially an old crock who used to loop bridges in a crate made of tissue and spit. Why take the risk, especially when greasing a civilian doesn't even bend the law? So it was strictly plan B, in case he couldn't be bought. If I croaked Strickling—assuming that wouldn't get me in Dutch with Emmett when he already had you digging up dirt—why'd I go to all this trouble to keep the cops out of it?"

It made sense; if anything surrounding a murder ever does. I put aside that line of reasoning, which was giving me a headache anyway.

I said, "You beat us both to the airfield with what you knew. What did you see while you were there?"

"Not as much as you did, brother. The lock on the door to the hangar gave me more trouble than I thought. I was still working on it when I heard the motor start up inside. I was making my way around to the front to check it out when I saw that spray of blood and decided it wasn't in my best interests to hang around; Yale's either. I went back the way I came, fixing to scale the fence behind the field to where I'd left the company car, when I saw the back door was open. Whoever started up that plane took off that way while I was gone."

"I don't buy it. You could squeeze a killer without worrying he'll go to the cops."

I was only half-listening to myself. I was thinking about that worn-out surveillance disc that had given up the ghost after Parrish started on the lock and before whoever had been inside—if someone *had* been inside—made his run. Everything Parrish said made sense, but I trusted him the way I trusted a floating craps game.

"Could," he said. "Kind of stupid to be telling you all this when I had a sweet deal like that all to myself."

Not if he was on a fishing expedition to find out how much I knew; but I didn't tip my hand. "What deal's that?"

"However much cash he had in that company folder he had with him. It sure wasn't an in-flight magazine. You don't make an appointment to fly over a border checkpoint without bringing along a deposit. The local TV folk got everything else on tape but that, even the lake of blood on the ground; which we won't see at six o'clock on account of the complaints that kind of thing always draws."

"It could've gotten chopped up along with his head."

He grinned. The corporation's insurance plan had given him a fine set of natural-looking teeth. "Stranger things have happened."

"Yale doesn't strike me as the kind to throw away money," I said. "Does he even know he's double-teaming Strickling?"

"A man's got to manage his own interests. After my boxing ticket got yanked I hung out my shingle: bodyguard work, most of it, but I picked up a trick or two. Enough anyway to land this gig, and beat you to the finish."

"You're counting on my not running to him with what you just told me. Nobody knows anybody that well."

When he narrowed his eyes, the puffy scar-tissue crowded them to the back of his head. "Go ahead, squeal on me. You think I did this because I'm afraid he's looking for new blood? I don't figure to stay around that long."

"Getting ready to pull the plug on a rich aunt?"

He looked cagy. "Let's just say I made up my mind when he started asking me to serve drinks to outside help."

I braced my hands on the arms of the chair. "I guess we're done here. Maybe you can sublet the place for the rest of the day."

"That's an idea, if they order dessert. We're counting pennies until we get this hitch worked out with our self-drivers. Personally I think Uncle Sam puts too much faith in bullshit technology; but what do I know? I'm just a rent-a-cop with an expense account."

I pushed myself up. He stretched out an arm and picked up the pistol. I froze in mid-crouch. Then he executed a neat Clint Eastwood twirl and squeaked it back into his shoulder clip.

"Keep the retainer. Strickling was the job."

I straightened. "Have your boss put it in writing. I'm still on the clock till then."

"You'll let us know if that money turns up. Legal will want to put in a claim if we can prove it's proceeds from a crooked stock deal based on a security leak. You might be in for a finder's fee." He was still smiling.

"I'll keep an eye out."

"Us too."

I left, and made all the usual turns back to the office without being aware of any of them. A big chunk of his story had fallen on my ears with all the pure clean chime of a rubber plug. He'd seen something the surveillance camera was too busy watching him to see; he'd practically bragged about it. As hunches go, that one was bottled in bond, but now wasn't the time to play it.

No one was parked in front of the building when I came out.

The officers had served their citation for the broken taillight and moved on to the next crime drama.

Which turned out to be me. I snatched the ticket from under the windshield wiper and filed it in the glove compartment, where it had company.

"You keep odd hours."

She'd made herself more comfortable on the yellow-oak pew in the waiting room than any of her predecessors, slipping off her shoes and sitting with her legs to one side, this time exposed by a black wraparound skirt like ballet dancers wear in rehearsal; it was an improvement over riding breeches and boots. With it she wore a snug peach-colored top with a boatneck that emphasized a really spectacular collarbone. Seated at an angle against the varnished-wood torture cage of a backrest, she spoke without looking up from the magazine she had spread open on the cushion beside her. Curious by nature as well as by profession, I craned my neck to check out her choice of reading material.

"*U.S. News and World Report,*" I said. "You heard me coming up the stairs. What are the odds that *People*'s still warm?" I pointed my chin at Scarlett Johansson pouting on the coffee table.

"You don't know me," Palm Volker said. "Don't try to prove you're that good of a detective." She lifted her lashes just enough to look at me from under them. They were pale compared to her hair and her eyes, still that tawny shade that warmed or cooled according to some internal thermostat. "I'm shut down until the FAA's done investigating. Since in the past ten days there was a twelve-passenger crash in Hawaii and a near-miss in Denver, I may not be back up and running till after the holidays; which I shouldn't have to tell you is the week that pays all next year's bills."

"That's the owner's headache, isn't it?"

"I'm the owner. Part, anyway."

"So you're the junior partner."

"The senior's Douglas, my ex. I'm flying under the radar. The TSA has to approve my buy-in. I had a close call when I was flying in Canada that's still under investigation, thanks to their celebrated socialist bureaucracy. With the police here, that makes three agencies breathing down my neck in two countries. I can't claim part proprietorship until I'm cleared, or Washington won't issue me a license." She slapped the magazine shut and swung her feet to the floor. They were long and slender like the rest of her. "I'm pouring out my secrets, Mr. Walker. You didn't even have to fire up the grill."

"I'm flattered. Why?"

"Quid pro quo. How much of what you told me about that dead man is good? I agreed to forego a generous divorce settlement in return for a junior interest, and used my life's savings to buy the property originally occupied by a shuttle service. Douglas's footing the bill for development and construction. If City Airport buys us out—and they're sniffing around—I'm set for life, but if I wind up damaged goods, I'm out on my ass. That means begging for a job behind the counter with some shit airline in some shit place like Guam. An unsolved murder at the airfield I'm in charge of pretty much guarantees that, with or without a clean bill of health from Ottawa."

"Why would that be?"

"No good reason; which is reason enough in the world of business and regulation, meaning Douglas Volker's world. He's the one with the green thumb when it comes to management: It's why I held my nose and went in with him. The watchdogs will demand a sacrifice, and I shouldn't have to tell you I'm the goat. So who killed Clare Strickling and why did it have to happen in my backyard?"

"What if I tell you what I know and it doesn't do you any good?"

"Then I'm no worse off. But at least I'll know just how bad off I am."

I shook loose the key to the private office. "Better put your shoes on. I haven't swept the floor since Easter."

SIXTEEN

My cell rang. I looked at the screen. It was Emmett Yale. I didn't answer. Seconds later, the landline went off. This time I didn't bother to look. It rang four times and stopped.

"Do you smoke?" I got one out and tapped it against the pack.

"You're the detective," Palm said. "Find a pilot who doesn't."

I reached the pack across the desk. She took one and leaned forward from her chair to let me light it. She blew a plume toward the window without inhaling. "Was that your client?"

I nodded. "Calling to end the association, I'm pretty sure. I saw the job through to the end according to the original terms. Actually, someone saw it through for me."

"Strickling?"

I didn't bother to answer that. I did bother to inhale.

"Stock manipulation's a white-collar crime," she said, "punishable by a couple of years in Club Fed. People don't commit murder at that level, or am I naïve?"

"People kill people over a Happy Meal."

"Different level."

I steered my thoughts away from the twenty thousand dollars burning a hole in my safe; the price of a one-way plane trip without pesky paperwork, or maybe just the down payment. Whatever

Strickling had cleared on the investment was as far outside my personal experience as a colony on Jupiter.

"I'll give you what I gave the cops." I told her about Yale, about suspecting his stepson Lloyd Lipton sold inside information to Strickling, about Lipton's killing soon after by Melvin Weatherall. "You've got the rest."

She'd laid her cigarette in the tray with one puff gone. "I read about that shooting. Do you think Weatherall—?"

"Not unless he knows how to slip an electronic tether. From what I saw, he couldn't change the batteries in a smoke detector. Rig an airplane up as a murder weapon?" I staggered out smoke. "Anyway, I'm convinced he didn't target Lipton. His kind drowns kittens and shoots at pretty cars just for the rush. Inspector Alderdyce doesn't buy the connection, and he's all cop. They make a habit of believing in coincidence; and I'm the Great Pumpkin."

"So why not answer the phone and punch out?"

"When someone dies unexpectedly, he leaves a lot of untidy things lying around. Somebody has to clean up."

"Why should that somebody be you?"

"It just is." Her cigarette was still smoldering in the tray. I put it out with the end of mine. "That's everything you asked for, footnotes and all. Satisfied?"

"Sure. And you're the Great Pumpkin." She got up and smoothed her skirt, awkwardly; she wasn't used to wearing one. "Drop in when you're ready to give me the rest."

"At work or at home?"

"Better make it at home. 'Private office'? There's no moron like an oxymoron."

Three stories down, her ancient Indian started up with a cough and a splutter and blatted away. I reached for the pack again, then decided to get away from the phone before it rang again. I turned off the cell and left.

There was no reason to visit the scene of another crime, especially one I'd made up my mind had nothing to do with what had happened to Clare Strickling. I wasn't even sure if Lipton was the one who sold insider information to him; if he was, that would make whoever killed Strickling harder to nail. But what made that my business? Certainly not the job I'd signed on for, and one that by any definition of the term was finished.

I should just go home, like everyone else at that hour who worked a normal day shift; leave work at the office where it belonged, fix a drink, and order a movie; a musical comedy or an animated feature, not *Chinatown*. But that twenty thousand kept me tied to the desk as securely as the bracelet on Melvin Weatherall's ankle. It had blood on it, even if it couldn't be seen. A lot of poor people could benefit from it. Detroit's a great place to be poor; it's a good-hearted sap of a town. It leads the country in food trucks, blankets, toys, shelters, and overcoats for the needy. An anonymous benefactor could lose himself in the crowd. But what if someone came calling for the money later, someone with a court order or a bludgeon or worse, a legitimate claim? I cranked up the big 455 and took I-75 north to the zoo, where Lloyd Lipton had died and started the chain of events that had led me to that hangar uptown.

Driving in a city I know so well is like floating in a sensory-deprivation tank; the practical part of the brain goes on autopilot, leaving the imagination free to roam. Something substantial had been drifting just beneath the surface most of the day, like a dark fish-shape in the shallows, too vague to identify. I wanted to wade in and slap it up onto the bank, the way bears do, but just the act of stirring the waters spooked it and it was gone. It came back now; I teased at it, trying to coax it to the surface.

The chill had set in for the night, and probably the week,

clouding the windshield. I switched the heater over to defrost. That broke the spell. The fish twitched its tail and swam away.

The Chrysler Freeway was moving at its usual pace for that time of day; if it slowed down just a little, it would be going backwards. I idled, I stopped, I sped up, I stood on the brakes six inches from the bumper in front of me. The water tower belonging to the zoo cruised into sight and stalled. It was always there, but it never seemed to get nearer. Our rush hours are measured in weeks. Beating them means going to work just as the bars are closing, driving past drunks weaving in the opposite direction.

I got hot, turned off the blower. Then I got cold and my breath stained the glass again. I switched back. This happened three times while we made ten yards. Horns honked; not from impatience, but from pure celebration whenever the traffic started moving again. If anyone here wasn't used to this, he must've been on a color tour from Miami. I switched on the radio and tuned in to the traffic band. A delay was announced. I switched it off.

Could be worse. There could be a Garth Brooks concert going on in Auburn Hills.

A Detroit blue-and-white sped past on the left shoulder, followed a moment later by a boxy ambulance and then a tow job pulling a flatbed trailer. That suggested an end to this ordeal, as well as the beginning of someone else's. I cracked my window and got a cigarette going off the dash lighter; tapped my horn button politely when the van in front of me lurched forward a couple of feet.

Finally things began to break up. The wreck cleared to the off-ramp and the emergency vehicles followed, without lights or sirens, meaning no one had been seriously injured in spite of the tangled mess of sheet metal on the flatbed trailer and the carpet of shattered glass glittering on the shoulder. I worked my way over to the exit, tossed out a couple more butts while waiting with the rest of the emigrants to lockstep our way through the changing lights at the end of the service drive, and swung out onto the four-lane road just as the streetlights came on.

Just before the overpass I turned in at a combination party store and service station, parked around the corner of the building down from the air hose, and got out. There was no pedestrian sidewalk. I kept to the grass berms, skipping over the iron-and-concrete drains in the ditches and avoiding the litter that collected there like flotsam at low tide. No doubt I attracted my share of attention from the motorists whipping past; nobody with an ounce of self-preservation walks in that area, especially with darkness pushing in; but nobody with a knowledge of our modern world pulls over to offer assistance to a stranded party either, so apart from stoplights at crossings I continued without interruption.

I paused on the approach to the overpass to peer over the railing, at the stretch of roadway I'd driven on minutes before. I'd stepped into a mirror and was looking out. I'd never been to that part of the greater sprawl except on wheels, and now instead of gazing up at the cantilevered yards of concrete flanking the freeway I was looking down from the top; it was dizzying, like standing on the edge of an industrial dam staring down the long white sweep to the bottom. The rampart at my feet seemed steeper than it did from below.

It must have been like this for a defender in chain-mail standing between battlements on a wall protecting a medieval city. The cars, trucks, and buses moved in singles and tandem, this way and that, manipulated by an outside force like beads in an abacus. The postwar city architects had designed the spanking-new concrete arteries to serve double-duty as drainage ditches: a plan that must have looked dandy on the drafting table, but when the spring rains came bore a closer resemblance to Genesis 7.

I pushed myself away and turned the corner onto the pedestrian walkway, separated from the whirl of traffic by a steel railing. The gridwork beneath my feet vibrated constantly, numbing the soles. It was strewn with butts, plastic- and Styrofoam cups, paper sacks with their suspicious contents, and small crumpled cardboard boxes—Marlboros; the teenage boys' shortcut of choice to rugged manhood. The usual driftwood pile of beer cans at the base of traffic signs, convenient targets unscarred by the invariable misses. At 70 m.p.h. there was no reason to look back at your effluvia.

I stopped halfway across I-75 and looked down again, gripping the outside railing with both hands. It was cold and rough, like a rusty pump handle.

It was as good a place as any. Here, give or take a couple of yards either direction, Melvin Weatherall had stood, taken aim at the first likely prospect, a sporty model he'd never own and, grinning with concentration, pressed the trigger. For him it was no different from throwing a beer can at a road sign. From atop city walls the cars were just pieces of moving metal, offering no hint of the squirming lives inside. The report would have been lost in the thrum of tires, the man-made gale of restless incessant movement. For the witnesses there would be only tearing rubber two stories below, a vehicle spinning across lanes, triggering a chain of low-velocity collisions in the sluggish flow. That there should be only one casualty was pure chance.

What were they thinking, those city planners? Why provide an accommodation for people to stand on foot between two steady streams of motor vehicles, laid out at two different levels? Flesh and steel were never intended to mingle. The monotonous motion on both sides created an eerie illusion: The earth was turning at an accelerated rate while I held on, gripping the railing until my knuckles wanted to burst, holding fast against gusts from the passing cars trying to send me sailing over the top. You didn't appreciate the speed they were traveling until you stood stock-still within a few feet of the rushing metal: It was a lesson in relativity. I swayed; my head swam. I turned away and tried to fire up a cigarette, but my hands shook and the slipstream blew out three matches before I could raise a spark. I gave up. I went back the way I came, collar up, fists stuck deep in my pockets. The air from above and below was icy. The seasons were changing.

The cops were waiting for me when I got back to my car, guns drawn.

SEVENTEEN

s it all right if I go over it again one more time?" I said. "Just to make sure my story doesn't change?"

But the detective sergeant, a trim black in a charcoal three-piece and gold-rimmed glasses, was one of the new breed: You can expose yourself only to so much kvetching on Facebook, Snapchat, TikTok, and all the other time-cannibals before you develop a Teflon coat impervious to irony; a kind of counter-cynicism, like an anti-missile missile. In a flat tone he said, "No need. We've got a positive from an eyewitness placing you on the scene at the right time. We're just shooting the breeze till the inspector gets here."

I glanced at the wide mirror that wasn't fooling anyone. I learned more from his questions than he did from my answers, including why I was there. A defense attorney wouldn't score any points hammering at Edna North-Flagg's dependency on corrective lenses during cross-examination; she'd read the name on my ID in the split-second I'd exposed her to it back at Golden Eagle Excursions, retained it long enough to report it to the police, and if the sergeant wasn't bluffing had recognized me through the two-way glass from the hallway outside the interview room. Professional wing-walkers don't survive to collect Social Security without a cool head and a keen sense of judgment.

It would have been a sprint from her 911 call to my license plate on file to a pair of cruising officers spotting it on their way past the service station off I-75. I still hadn't been told who I'd killed, but young Herbie Hancock here had dropped enough hints to form the connection, hoping I would slip up and make his case before the brass arrived and claimed star billing. But he'd given up on that with as much good grace as he could scrounge, like a weary school counselor who'd failed to get through to his charge and blamed the student for his failure.

Gabe Parrish and I had had a moment there back at Golden Eagle Excursions; now he was dead, and I hardly knew him. And I was the last one to see him alive, at least according to the record as it stood.

We were in one of the smaller rooms set aside for the purpose. I didn't think I'd been in it before, but the mustard-colored walls, printed woodgrain table on a steel trestle, high-school cafeteria chairs, and imitation-marble-imitation-linoleum floor came in bulk lots, varying only according to the specific chips in the plastic veneer and the finger smudges on the light switch. For all I knew I had been brought here every time. It wouldn't be a Kodachrome memory.

I wondered what time it was. I'd been forced to surrender my wristwatch at the admissions desk along with my wallet, ID folder, pocket change, and keys, and the kind of time that passes in custody can't be measured in circadian terms. It was probably getting on toward midnight. They don't feed you until you're actually in a cell, so the gnawing in my stomach suggested a timeline from the barbecue I'd had before my session with Melvin Weatherall and the two beers I'd had at his place to be sociable. The sergeant shot his cuff from time to time to look at the circle of gold on his wrist, but he didn't share the results. That was supposed to make me break down and confess, in return for a report on the current position of the earth in its rotation; but that lab experiment involves days in limbo, not a couple of hours. He wasn't letting anything in the department manual of interrogation go unexploited. I didn't ask. It was a war of wills.

Finally a knuckle grazed the door and he opened it to exchange murmurs with someone outside. He swung the door wide on the uniform standing there. "Go with this officer."

I got up and gave an upper arm to the whipsaw figure in blue. He smelled of English Leather and cornstarch. I hoped I'd see the sergeant again, if only because his cool-jazz look was a change of scenery in that place. I bet he sat in at the Chord Progression every Saturday night.

The layout there is a rabbit warren of identical L-shaped hallways like a family medical clinic, so I couldn't be sure, but I thought John Alderdyce had been shunted to a different office since my last visit. The DPD had broken city precedent by appointing him to a consultancy after a few months of uneasy retirement, so accommodations had to be shifted until he'd settled someplace where he wouldn't get in the way of routine police business. This one was the standard rectangle with generic artwork on the Sheetrock walls and a gray steel desk, although he'd adjusted it to his comfort with an area rug in a geometric pattern and a caramel-colored Naugahyde sofa I remembered from before. When my escort discharged his responsibility and closed the door behind me, the inspector was seated on one hip on the corner of the desk. It was never a good sign when he affected a casual attitude. He was as informal as a state dinner at the White House; any deviation from the norm was window-dressing, designed to throw the observer off balance.

Just knowing that should have provided some comfort, but even that was part of the strategy. He made Niccolò Machiavelli look like Nick the Greek.

I'd never before seen him in the same suit three times in succession, or wearing a shirt not as crisp as a fresh fall of snow;

but I remembered with a shock that it was the same day, the one that had begun with Clare Strickling alive. Some days travel like that, strapped on the back of a tortoise with a club foot. Plainly Alderdyce had thrown his morning layout back on after he'd been called back in to look at yet another corpse. His collar was open and his necktie at half-mast, possibly in respect for the departed but more likely because he needed to save the effort for more important things. His face confirmed that. It was like coming across a familiar figure unexpectedly, seeing it without the filter of intimacy. He looked his age, and consequently I knew I looked mine.

"Don't you ever go home?" he said.

I said, "You're the second person today to question the hours I keep. I'm not a civil servant like you. What's your excuse?"

He twisted to scoop a manila envelope off the desk. The flap was open. The eight-by-ten photographs inside slid out when he tipped it, shingling across the composition top.

It was an invitation. I picked them up, pushed them together, and shuffled through them. The department shutterbugs had converted to digital, but the darkroom techs were still using the grainy black-market stock laid in before V-J Day. Still, the body sprawled in that telltale bent-limb position had been obliging enough to fall faceup, so it didn't have to be flipped for identification; it had that bundle-of-sticks look that can't be arranged.

On the evidence of the burst swivel lying nearby on its back, Emmett Yale's head of security had been sitting when the bullet shattered his breastbone, catapulting him back and over and making a stain on his white-on-white shirt like a lopsided star, his undecorative black tie pasted to the shirt by blood, as square and straight as in a studio shot, a comical effect the ex-prizefighter wouldn't have approved. The chair's wheels would have made a few useless revolutions in the air after his heart had stopped.

I separated one from the rest and turned it his way. "This one does him the most justice."

"Meaning you recognize him."

"Gabe Parrish. He was chief cop at Yale Mobility." I laid the sheaf on the desk. "He said he rigged our meeting at Golden Eagle to convince me he didn't kill Strickling. But you know that; they wire these rooms for a reason."

"How is it he knew you knew he's a suspect and we didn't?"

"Don't be greedy, John. You've got enough to hang on me without that, and it won't wash. You had everything I did: assuming you saw the same video Palm Volker showed me."

"She showed us several. The stuff from the cameras trained on the front of the hangar was inconclusive. The construction crew kept cutting the underground power lines. All we got from the back was half a disc and an unidentifiable party monkeying with the lock. After that someone ran over the disc with the Third Armored Division and the rest was blank. Why make the investment in security and cut corners on the software?"

"Palm made the same complaint. The party wasn't so unidentifiable if you'd ever seen him walk. Parrish boxed professionally; he said he had a license for a while. Long enough anyway to pick up that rolling gait, halfway between Popeye the Sailor and a fiddler crab. The balls of the feet wear out before the heels."

Alderdyce looked as contented as he ever got, waiting for the other shoe to drop. "So we can close the case on Strickling," he said. "Except why he was worth killing and what story this Parrish gave you that got you to lay off."

"I laid off? I thought I killed him. The sergeant said."

"The sergeant's in a hurry to make lieutenant. He doesn't know how well off he is. How'd you spend the rest of your day if you didn't buy Parrish's story? You were hired to prove Strickling sicced Weatherall on Lloyd Lipton to cover up a Wall Street beef. You put that to rest when you eliminated Weatherall as anything but a bag of shit with a gun and too much time on his hands. Once you'd placed Parrish at the scene of the Strickling kill, all you had to do was come to us with it, trusting this here well-oiled machine of justice to whomp up a mess of evidence out of nothing while you fly off to rescue some other Lois Lane. How long do I know you? You don't take your teeth out of someone's leg unless he offers you a bone with more meat on it. What was it?"

Just then that dark shape darted past down in the murk. I slapped at the water. I missed the big fish, but I didn't come up entirely empty-handed.

"A brainstorm," I said. "More of a drizzle; but you can't pick them. He said he didn't see anything, but he was too smug for somebody with nothing to sell. That wasn't what bothered me, though; it was something else. I went to that overpass looking to reel it in. You know the vibe you sometimes get from a conversation about something else entirely: nothing you can bring to court, but a nudge in a likely direction. I saw something on Parrish's face when I walked into Jack Flagg's office, a flicker in his eyes. At the time I thought it was just annoyance; I was earlier than expected, before he had time to put on his game face. Now I think it was surprise. I wasn't the visitor he was expecting."

"Who was?"

"Whoever started up that propeller that took Clare Strickling's head off his body. He knew who it was, and he was looking to collect."

A strong set of teeth worried at his cheek. He slid off the desk, circled behind it, and used a key from the reel on his belt to unlock a drawer. He dumped out another manila envelope. My .38 and the stuff from my pockets spilled across the desk.

"Parrish was killed with a nine-millimeter," he said. "Jacketed slug, probably from a semiautomatic, which you never carry. I could hold you another sixty-six hours and change on suspicion, but I didn't come back to work in this shithole just to roll logs. I'll make you a present of those hours, for which I confidently and aggressively expect a full statement when they're up; and it better come with something we can use. Otherwise that Magnum we got from the search warrant at your place turns up wherever we misplaced it in the evidence room and you can face a license review board in Lansing—after you serve your time for possession of an unregistered handgun."

"I almost forgot I had the damn thing. My grandmother gave it to me on her deathbed. She fought Indians with it."

"We ran it: It's so clean it has to be dirty. Your grandmother chose the wrong side." He watched me distribute the items on my person. "Your heap's in the impound on Michigan. Need a ride?"

"I'd appreciate it."

"You're in luck. The last pay phone in the city's just outside in the hall."

EIGHTEEN

I was flying without instruments, also without wings or a motor. My Lewis gun was jammed, and when I tried to clear it, it fell overboard. That left me with no way to defend myself against a barrage of enemy planes that swooped down from the sun, buzzing like yellowjackets and trying to cut my hair with their propellers. I ducked and cringed and tried to go into a dive; but really, all you can do when you're strapped to a doghouse is sit there and shake your fist at the Red Baron. I woke up actually doing that. An autumn-orange sun was edging above the windowsill in my bedroom.

It was no rest at all, and no more than I deserved. *Work* is defined as labor that accomplishes something, and all I'd managed to do on the longest day I'd put in since the Persians took Damascus was kill a couple of beers and get myself arrested. It wasn't my first time, but usually I manage that much before lunch.

I shuffled out into the kitchen, where the coffeemaker pouted at me on the counter; I'd charged it and forgotten to activate the timer. While it gurgled I sorted through the greasy crumples of brown paper on the table, looking for nutritious crumbs. I'd grabbed a couple of doughnuts and a paper cup of paintstrip at an all-night place on the way home from the police impound lot, but it sure wasn't Krispy Kreme: It gave me indigestion and left me just as hungry. I fried the last strip of bacon from the package and crunched it while I brought in the morning *Free Press,* and all the while the carafe was filling like an hourglass with a broken mainspring.

The circumstances of Clare Strickling's death were enough of a departure from the daily dish of homicide to claim a piece of the front page with a jump to page 3 and a photo of the Piper, nose down and tail up like a ducking-waterbird. The reporter, a veteran newshawk I knew slightly, had gotten most of the details right, but laid out in the fast-vanishing pyramid they read like the results of a cricket match in Grimsby-on-the-Humber; certainly nothing that had anything to do with me, and didn't contribute a speck to what I'd heard on the radio last night. I wasn't mentioned.

I did get some ink in the City section. "A local private investigator" was being questioned in the case of a fatal shooting in the historic Healy Building; but if not for that landmark the piece wouldn't have gotten even the three inches that appeared without a byline.

The phone rang just as the coffee finished brewing. I carried the mug into the living room, said "One moment, please," into the receiver, slurped, and said, "Okay, but start easy."

"Walker?"

The familiar voice sounded like a recording played back at slow speed. I kicked mine up to compensate.

"Good morning, Mr. Yale. How are things in Galveston?"

"How is anything anywhere? Something else always comes up. You fix a drawer and the refrigerator stops working. You settle a strike, then fly home to learn your security chief's been killed and the man you hired to solve your stepson's murder did it. I'm assuming that's you. This thing won't support two private eyes."

"It barely supports one; but I'm used to clipping coupons.

Anyway, that was yesterday. Today someone else did it. Tomorrow I may be a suspect again, in a different murder. I'm averaging two a day at present."

"What does any of this have to do with Melvin Weatherall?"

"About as much as it has to do with labor unrest in Texas. He's clean—of shooting Lipton for any reason other than rotten bloodlust. I'm not even sure it was your stepson who sold that information to Strickling."

Air crackled in a soundproof room. "Are you actively trying to get me to say your services are no longer required?"

"Passively; but from the bottom of my heart." I drank more coffee. It didn't live up to the amount of anticipation I'd invested. Nothing ever does.

"I don't dismiss employees over the phone. You know where my office is?"

"No," I lied. That *employee* crack wouldn't get to me if it came with a dental plan.

"You're a detective. Look it up. I'll expect you in an hour."

I listened to the dial tone. Lately it seemed everyone was telling me I'm a detective. You can only hear that so many times before you begin to wonder.

NINETEEN

This one had me running on a continuous loop, like one of those plastic horses pegged into grooves on a toy track. It had been almost exactly twenty-four hours since I'd dropped in on Clare Strickling in his apartment in Saline, and here I was back in the neighborhood.

Yale had dozed the barns and stock pens on the county fairgrounds, erected a space-age city bordering a composition oval track on three sides, and trucked in gravel and dirt on the north end, working it up into hills, grades, and dips representing every variety of terrain on the North American continent; his landscapers even took plaster casts of teeth-shattering potholes from existing rural roads and replicated them on-site. That way his designers and mechanics were able to put their axles, suspensions, and tie rods through their paces under actual road conditions and make adjustments as necessary. Every day except Christmas and Labor Day, the bawling of engines and meshing of gears thundered out across a countryside where livestock had bleated and lowed and half-forgotten country stars had warbled all their old hits, drawing much the same complaint from the non-participating neighbors; but Yale had addressed that by assuming all the construction costs of a sound-retention wall around the track and along the state road and donating a half-million-dollar aquarium to the local marine research center.

A billboard-size sign advertised the place in letters slanted to the right at a thirty-degree angle, as if leaning into the wind:

> YALE MOBILITY
> "Where Hope Meets Promise"
> E.M. Yale, Prop.

The layout was a city in every way, except for the absence of a democratic system of government. It had its own fire department and police force, electrical plant independent of Detroit Edison and Consumers Energy, a rail system that made Amtrak/Conrail look like the amateur enterprise it was, and a self-elected mayor for life in the person of Emmett Yale, former GM draftsman and board member and now the sole owner of a business whose treasury needn't blush in the presence of the United Kingdom.

A diagonally striped gate barred the entrance to the grounds. The ex-jarhead in the booth found my name on his electronic clipboard and reached a plastic visitor's card through my window. "Hang it on your pocket. You wear it anywhere but the administration building, you'll find yourself in detention."

"You're buttoned down that tight?"

"Always, but more today. We just lost our chief of security." He raised the gate.

The grounds were laid out like a medical campus, in a grid with sidewalk-lined streets and signs on the corners directing visitors to the various offices and divisions (Research & Development, Public Safety, Glass Plant, Infirmary, and finally Administration), each with its own parking lot.

I pushed the posted 15 m.p.h. speed limit; I was a few minutes late. The change in the weather had laid down a ground fog that had stalled in mid-rise, decreasing visibility, slowing the already sluggish rush, and reducing visibility to an abstraction of head-lamps, taillights, and stuttering brake signals all along the route. I slowed at the intersections, swiveling the spotlight mounted on the fender to read the signs.

But I was distracted by more than just the poor visibility.

As I'd turned off the state road, a car that had been crawling behind me continued past, and I saw that one of its taillights was out. That bottom-dwelling fish I'd been stalking off and on swam just past my line of sight; when I tried to look at it directly it flashed away. It was an important fish or it wouldn't keep coming back to tease me. It must have been a whopper.

The administration building looked like all the rest, a triple-decker sandwich of black tempered glass and steel, accessed by a single revolving door, with cameras installed on the roof corners at overlapping angles. At the first sign of trouble, the door would lock automatically, trapping the visitor between the angled panes like a firefly in a jar. Here where hope met promise there would be no power interruptions, no worn-out recording discs, nothing slipshod about protecting industrial secrets in the most compet-itive enterprise since the Arms Race; Gabe Parrish would have seen to that. The quest for his successor would be like electing a new pope.

I cruised past a line of shining Yale autos parked in slots with the names of executives stenciled on the curb in descending or-der of rank, looking for a space in the visitors' section. Yale's name was absent; a chauffeur-driven town car would come for him when he called, and Parrish's spot was as empty as a haunted house. At length I pulled in next to a proletarian Chevy—like me, a refugee outsider—got out, and hiked to the entrance. The fog was lifting now, grumpily, the mercury lights atop the fifteen-foot poles glimmering through it, as remote as the moons of Saturn.

Curved stucco walls enclosed the foyer, turning it into a cavern.

A woman sat inside the doughnut hole of a centrally located desk that seemed to exist only to support a trivet reading ADMISSIONS; but that didn't appear to be promising anything. She wore blue serge and a haircut that made the skinhead guard at the gate look like a fugitive from Woodstock. She spoke my name into a claymore-shaped handset she took from a shelf under the counter and pushed a button that opened a seamless door in the curved wall. It moved without sound; the only thing in the room less noisy than the woman who manipulated it.

No directions were necessary. A Lubyanka-type hallway extended the entire depth of the building, lit by recessed fixtures and carpeted with some Astroturf-like substance that gave underfoot like flesh. The walls, too, were manmade of an absorbent material and bore no ornament of any kind. The stretch was absolutely silent; I felt that I could shout at the top of my lungs and not even hear myself. Everything was the same gunmetal shade. Extending as long as it did, the passage was disorienting; dizzying, like weightless space. I was enclosed, but the sensation was like walking across a football field, exposed to the world. There would be cameras mounted behind some type of mesh that concealed them without obstructing the view of whoever sat at the monitors. The Pentagon was more penetrable and less hostile to the eye; but then it had to deal with the press, and Yale Mobility was hermetically sealed against public opinion. The design of the ashtrays in next year's Yale electric were safe, at least from me.

I reached the only door in a mile without dropping from dehydration. It was blank and set flush, so that I might have overlooked it if it weren't bare steel, textured differently from the wall. It lacked either knob or handle. Something clunked and it opened inward on noiseless hinges. That confirmed my hunch about surveillance cameras.

I expected an airlock, another example of impedimenta to postpone the suspense of a face-to-face with Il Duce, but I was standing inside an office not quite as large as the VIP box where we'd met in Cleveland, back when Caesar was courting Cleopatra; or was it last week? But it wasn't built to intimidate. It needed space for the occupant to pass between a pedestal desk of no particular style and a stout square table the size of my garage, with a hole in the middle, also square, like the ones model railroad enthusiasts use to gain access to their elaborate layouts; the layout in this case being a space-age complex of domed and conical miniature buildings connected by enclosed elevated walkways, the kind that link airport terminals to parking structures, made of molded plastic or something as remote from natural elements. It was all a uniform shade of eggshell and there wasn't a right angle or a corner in the whole expanse.

"A pipe dream," said a familiar voice; "but soon to become a reality. It's to be entirely self-contained, like the old Ford River Rouge plant, but immune to the anti-trust laws, if the Constitutional scholars on the payroll can be relied on. It's gone through four architects and started from scratch every time. I had to scrap anything that resembled a skyscraper in order to mollify the cracker-barrel crowd."

Emmett Yale had exchanged weekend wear for business dress, the same gray as the corridor outside except for a lighter gray shirt, mauve necktie, and glistening black patent-leather shoes, and his iron-gray hair was brushed back as neatly as before; but the man himself didn't look as fresh as his clothes. He had carry-on bags under his eyes and his frown pulled deep furrows down from his nostrils. It had little to do with age, and possibly nothing more to do with worry. A man with half his years would look the same after three hours in the air and I was guessing less than that in bed. This time he didn't offer his hand.

I said, "What's a town sell for these days? I don't keep up."

"It wasn't as bad as all that. The city needed a senior recreation center; and the city manager needed an in-ground pool. This is all part and parcel of our professional confidence, Walker. If the good public servants of Saline suspect I'm relocating, our tax benefits will dry up before we can finish construction."

"No worries. I don't work for politicians. They won't pay up front, and they never pay after they lose an election. How was your flight?"

"First class isn't what it was, and the stewardesses dress like CPAs. Who shot Parrish?"

The small-talk portion of the morning was over. He tipped a callous-fingered hand in the direction of a brown leather tiltback chair. I pretended I didn't see it and pulled up a padded upright with arms. Charles Eames hadn't had my sacroiliac. Yale took that one and crossed his legs. The bottom curve of his calves under the black socks was almost as thick as his late bodyguard's. Caesar's nose or not, anyone who didn't know who he was would take him for a retired shop steward; certainly not a man who'd founded an empire sitting at a drafting table.

The room's back wall was glass and looked out on the rest of the campus, including the sound-resistant wall encircling the test track. Despite that bulwark, I'd heard the engines roaring on the way to the building, although muted; here it was nonexistent. The window had to be triple-paned, with colorless gas creating buffers in between. Yale had hired me under just those conditions back at the ballpark, in a goldfish bowl with a panoramic view and the chatter from the announcer's booth turned off. It wasn't a goldfish bowl. It was a combination command post and war room; all it lacked were the model tanks and toy soldiers on the table. To-day's Pattons and Churchills conduct their campaigns in just such places, without uniforms or casualty counts.

Anyway, without uniforms.

"Not my call," I said. "I hired on to find the bridge between Weatherall and Strickling if there was one. I'm satisfied there isn't. What happened to Lloyd Lipton was more on the order of a natural disaster, if you lump human dregs like Melvin Weatherall in with earthquakes and mudslides; not my area at all. What happened to Parrish ties in more than likely with what happened to Strickling, and even more likely still had nothing to do with your stepson's death. I already told you I'm not even sure he's the one who tipped off Sterling you were buying up computer chips like a two-for-one sale at Costco. Impressive as they are, the measures you and Parrish took to protect Yale Mobility's secrets from the outside are no protection against threats from inside."

"Granted that—and I'm not prepared to accept that Lloyd's murder was a random act—you must have a theory about Parrish's, even if it's just a guess." He held up one of his expressive palms before I could open my mouth. "If you're afraid my security system includes a recording device in this office, don't be. If I'm a suspect, snagging you in a defamation-of-character suit wouldn't bring me any benefit."

"I don't suspect anyone. That takes time I'm not being paid for. Anyway, my gut feeling involves a dead man, who according to the U.S. Supreme Court has no rights in law." I told him about Parrish's reaction when I walked in on him in the Healy Building.

He said nothing when I paused, showed nothing in the way of keen anticipation. His face would be just that blank in business meetings when a subordinate suggested changing the cutlery in the executive dining room.

"I think he knew who killed Strickling," I said; "he either guessed or saw something, maybe even the killer in action, and set up the appointment to work a squeeze. That's who he was expecting when he commandeered Jack Flagg's office, and it's who killed him when he made his pitch."

Outside the window, a Stealth-shaped auto painted schoolbus-yellow with a big numeral 9 emblazoned on the door came cruising around the curve of the baffled wall that surrounded the track, headed toward a single-story building with multiple bays, presumably a charging station. Yale didn't turn to look at it.

He shook his head. "I've been in commerce too long to believe anyone's incapable of blackmail, but I don't see the percentage to Parrish. No security director in the country was paid better; and I'm not excluding the head of the Secret Service. Granted there might be seven figures involved in this stock deal, but was he so sure he could cut himself in he'd risk losing a fat steady salary? That's supposing the murderer somehow got a piece of it, which we haven't discussed."

Parrish had been interested enough to bring up the subject of that money; but I didn't argue. I still had no idea who held title to the twenty thousand in my safe—a deposit, nothing more, on private airfare to a safer place; there would be plenty more in reserve—and Yale might press me for it, thinking it was owed him because of the leak. I did a soft shoe.

"Drawing a paycheck and sitting on a cushion of undeclared income don't carry the same weight. He said he was getting restless. What's sexier than a suitcase full of cash no one knows anything about?"

"No one," he said, "except whoever has it now, or has a line on it. I'm not convinced Weatherall didn't have a hand in this, but even if you're right, I don't want to encourage anyone to use a business I raised from a pup to profit from a despicable crime. So if you have no objections, you're still on the payroll. Having invested twice in murder, why would he stop?"

I was grinning, I could tell. My face felt like it was in a cast. "Well, don't sugarcoat it," I said.

TWENTY

told him he was knee-deep in chiselers already. Why not let the system take its course?

"A better question is, why do you insist on talking yourself out of gainful employment—unless all these corpses have got you rattled?"

My grin this time came naturally. "Scared stiff, Mr. Yale; but nice try."

He spent a few seconds deciding whether to get mad. Finally he nodded.

"Okay, so your ego is impregnable. Mine isn't. A killer has thumbed his nose at me—at me, not just my company!—and I'm damned if I'll leave him to the authorities. The case could wind up in the lap of a feeble specimen like Judge Kitchner, and who will I hire to rectify *that* miscarriage of justice? Who would Moses?"

"Moses had ten laws to enforce," I said. "Kitchner does the best he can with two hundred fat volumes compiled by public servants. If it's a rat terrier you want, someone who'll follow our killer down his hole and finish him off clean, find another dog. The city's full of 'em—if you're lucky enough not to draw an undercover cop instead of Icepick Charlie; otherwise you'll find out just how feeble the Kitchners of this world are. Your world *and* mine," I added.

He spread his communicative hands.

"We're fellow independents, you and I. We've got nothing to distract us from sewing a straight stitch; no bosses running for re-election, no press turning up the heat, no outraged citizens' committees storming the front door with petitions. I've got a team of technicians whose continued employment depends exclusively on finding out why our self-driving cars don't drive themselves: and if you take my offer, finding whoever murdered Gabe Parrish—who was *my* man, so far as the world is concerned—and making sure a charge of Murder One sticks all the way to a life sentence—well, you won't find me ungrateful." He drew that silver tablet from an inside breast pocket and started thumbing buttons.

I stood up.

"I'd have saved you the sermon," I said, "but everyone needs to blow off steam now and then. I wasn't satisfied with the way the job turned out myself. We'll work out payment when I come through—or don't. Meanwhile, what you put in my account on the Strickling deal will stand my expenses until I have to charter a jet."

I left then. The day was still young, but I wasn't, and the job was expanding in indirect ratio to my abilities. Finding Parrish's killer was a tall enough order in itself. Now that he was more than likely on his way to a hat trick, it was twice as tall. Whoever it was was just hitting his stride, and I was already two steps behind.

It broke the surface with a crash; that vague dark shape sounded suddenly, like a hooked trout, and hit me square between the eyes.

The fog had lifted—a poetic turn for a climactic normality—and a tangerine autumn sun had dried up the last of the lingering puddles. I had a high-definition view of the traffic in the rearview, including a lime-colored Suburban three cars back.

After the shock of recognition I smiled. I knew it would be

missing its left taillight assembly. I'd seen that heap twice before; three times, if I was right about the vehicle that had passed me when I turned into the auto complex, based on its single red lens. The second time had been down the street from the Healy Building just the day before, being ticketed for a safety violation. I blamed the delay in making the connection on age; it had taken Old Sol himself to bring light into my thickening skull.

Playing follow-the-leader is always a treat. Usually it gives me an opportunity to show off my talent for losing unwanted company. This time I gave the shadow a break. He wasn't adept or I wouldn't have spotted him in the first three blocks, so I helped him out, slowing as I approached the yellow lights so I wouldn't leave him stuck at the stops. That took a different kind of skill, like a pool shark hustling the rubes or a junior executive muffing a putt so the boss could catch up, and making it look genuine.

The intention was to work my way behind him and get a look at his plate. I happen to be good at that, in a town I know as well as mine. I stopped for gas, for cigarettes, and a Sausage McMuffin, hoping he'd do what he had at Yale: cruise past, wait, and pick me up again when I got back on the road; but he was either on to that or lucky. Each time I didn't pick him up again until he hove into sight in my mirror.

All the way back to Detroit we were practically the only two cars on the freeway obeying the speed limit. It was a wonder we weren't both nipped for holding up the mid-morning commute.

Despite everything, all my genius at the wheel, I almost lost him at the I-75 interchange when a double-bottom rig changed lanes behind me, blocking his view of my turn signal; a shriek of brakes told me he'd woken up just in time to take advantage of a traffic gap the size of a fruit cup, taking three lanes at a sixty-degree angle on the outside of his tires. He was as green as his ride; but that was his ace. You can't predict what an amateur will do in a crunch. He caught up with me on Woodward. After that he wasn't taking any chances. He stuck to my rear bumper like what was left of the chrome.

Now that I was back on a surface street I tried again. I slid into the curb, pretending I had a call that was too important to split my attention between it and the road. He swung into a driveway a block back. By the time I got turned around to follow, he'd ducked into an alley or around another corner. Back on the main route he popped up again like a No Sale tab; behind me, always behind.

I lost patience; it was like trying to hold up a bum opponent long enough to take a dive in the ring. I accelerated. The bus lane came between us. He was on his own now.

Anyway I had another arrow in my quiver.

The breather was temporary, and just pique, because unless he was a complete idiot he knew where I was headed. I drove the rest of the way to the office without paying any special attention, parked in my custom spot across from the office, and climbed upstairs to tap the bottle and place a call.

It took a few minutes to track down John Alderdyce, who answered with his mouth full.

"Swallow first," I said. "You might choke on this one."

He swallowed. "Funny thing about this phone. Every time a bell rings, an angel gets it in the neck; when it's you calling."

That one was way out of season, but I let him keep it. "I need to check on a ticket issued yesterday afternoon on Woodward; not to me. You wouldn't fix it if I were Smokey Robinson."

"You need to recognize a joke when you hear one, Walker. I never was with Stationary Traffic. I started out on the old Tactical Mobile Unit. I even got to drive first day, rising star that I was."

"Hell, everyone knows about that. It's the cop behind the wheel who takes the first bullet in an ambush."

"So they told me when I bragged about it back in the locker room. To what do my ulcers owe this call?"

"This one's a moving violation, not overdue parking. What I'm after is a citation for a broken taillight."

I took advantage of a string of language forbidden by Department HR to lay the receiver on the desk and light a cigarette, then got back on when he paused for breath. "I'm not trying to fix a ticket, John. You might beat a homicide rap, but it's the traffic fines that keep the city in the black. This guy's good for both."

TWENTY-ONE

Anyone who didn't know John Alderdyce—and who did?—would have trouble separating the set of blasphemies he employed to manage his anger from the set he used to express satisfaction. My telephone ear was still numb two minutes after I rang off. I barely heard the buzzer that warned me a visitor had entered the outer office.

It could've been the mail carrier, but there was the outside chance the driver of the green Suburban had decided to take his fine for a moving violation out of my hide, with the same piece he'd used on Parrish. I separated the .38 from the small of my back, laid it on the desk with my hand resting on it, and called out an invitation.

Tailspin Tommy came in like a human pinwheel, twirling all the way around on his toes as he shut the door behind him. He wore a brown leather bomber jacket with a sheepskin collar and the elbows frayed almost through, baggy whipcords, elastic-sided ankle boots built up at the heels, and a black felt beret clinging for its life to the side of a bald head spotted with age. A yellowed silk scarf went twice around his neck, trailing its fringed end down the side of his hollow chest. Glass-blue eyes glittered through folds of skin behind black-rimmed glasses with lenses as big around as .45 rpm records. A not-unpleasant odor came in with him: a combination of dried-out cornhusks and Juicy Fruit gum. He was as bow-legged as a Chippendale chest and as old as the High Lama of Shangri-La.

I opened the belly drawer of the desk and slid the gun into it. He stared at me; not because of the action—that made as much of an impression on him as the annual mean rainfall in Brazil—but because of the look I must have worn on my face.

"What's so funny?" His voice snapped with the high percussive force of a firecracker.

I pushed back my chair and stood. "Don't take it personally. I was expecting someone unwelcome. Have a seat, Major."

"You seen my act?" The tone now was part caution, part suspicion. He was someone with a keen sense for ridicule; no doubt an acquired skill, but he didn't have to dress like that.

"Before my time," I said; "my loss. It was just a guess. Jack Flagg's Flying Circus: Thrills, chills, and all the cotton candy you can eat. I saw your posters. Is Mrs. Flagg okay? That was a nasty thing to come back to from lunch."

"Edna? She's a trouper, don't you worry about her. She fell sixty feet once onto hardpack; thermal ticked the wing. My fault: I over-compensated. She sprang up like a colt and finished the show. Didn't know till the next day her spine was cracked in three places."

"Sixty feet?"

He colored. It was like the rosy spread of flame through old newspaper. "Well, we didn't exactly have a tape measure handy. But X-rays is X-rays." He threw a leg over the customer's chair and perched on the edge, leaning forward with his hands clasped on his knees. The fingers were curled tight with arthritis. They looked like walnuts. "Wasn't you plugged that fella, was it?"

I shook my head and sat. "Just bad timing. What brings you here?"

"I'm to come fetch you. You're not answering your phone. We're practically neighbors, so she asked me to drop around."

"Who? Edna, the Wing-Walking Wizardess of the World? Who does she want to rat me out to this time, J. Edgar Hoover's ghost?" I checked my cell, which had turned itself off, something it did sometimes. Technology and I have never warmed to each other. I turned it back on and put it in my pocket.

"Not her. Pam."

"I don't know any Pams."

"Sure you do. Looks like Bergman, flies like Lindbergh. You'd don't forget a skirt like that. You one of them funny fellas?" When he squinted, his eyes vanished behind thickets of sun-cured skin.

"Palm," I spelled it. "Like the tree. Not Pam. Palm Volker. What does she want?"

"You seen her. Does it matter?"

"I'll get my hat." I got up again.

"What hat?" He aimed his bright eyes at the empty hall tree.

"Just a turn of phrase. Okay if I follow in my car?"

"Better drive slow. I didn't bring one."

"You walked all the way from the Healy Building?"

"Had to. There's no place around here to land."

Another colorful character. I should keep a scrapbook.

In the passenger's seat he stretched out his legs as straight as they would go and folded a strip of gum into his mouth. The pink wad bounced around in full view between the worn-down brown stumps of the last two of his molars.

"I let my license lapse ten years ago," he said. "It was either that or my pilot's ticket: Good luck prying that one out of one of these claws when I'm croaked. You know the way?"

"If it's the airfield."

"Where else? Back in Pyongyang I slept in the chopper. Never know who might monkey around with it when you ain't looking.

No real air-jockey goes home except to take a dump. Pam didn't lose her shirttail being stupid."

I didn't press for details. It would take me a semester at least to learn his language. "This is Detroit, not Korea."

"Not so's you'd notice. Anyways, she's got a business to get off the ground—off the ground, get it? That's a full-time job, I'm here to tell you."

There was no sign of my tail in lunch-rush traffic. The police hadn't had time to track down that citation on Woodward and act on it, so maybe I'd managed to lose him after all. Things should go that easy when I'm trying.

The slowdown gave me time for the conversation I wanted. "How much was Clare Strickling paying you to fly him out of the country?"

It was a stab in the dark, but it hit home.

"Depends on what you mean by paying. Grab two buckets, crap in one, promise in the other, see which one slops over first. Golden Eagle don't fly until there's money in its beak. Hell's bells! I ought to make that our slogan."

"But he arranged with you to make the flight?"

"Was to call when he had the cash. Twenty thousand smackers. I told all this once. Don't you cops talk to each other?"

"You saw where I work. Run into any uniforms there, guzzling Sam's Club Special Blend and complaining about their book-ies? I'm not a cop." I was getting the hang of the local dialect. "Where'd he want you to take him, Canada or Mexico?"

"Where you think? I should blow it all on fuel just for tacos and tequila?"

Getting answers meant picking through his questions. It was like grilling a contestant on *Jeopardy*. "When?"

"What are you, deaf as the old lady? I said he was to call. He better not make it collect from Purgatory. I sure won't accept the charges."

"Was anyone else authorized to take the money?"

"Just Edna. It wouldn't pass through my hands anyway. She's the bookkeeper, and she's tight as a hen's twat." Air stuttered out of his lungs, filling the car with strawberries and spearmint. I figured it was what he used for laughter.

"Who knew about it besides you three?"

"Like I'd drop a line to the IRS and declare a cash deal. You saw where *I* work. See any ticket machines, newsstands, pizza-by-the-slice joints, couple of dozen cute stewardesses in heat? I ain't Delta."

I was starting to like the old son of a bitch; I hated that. "Any chance someone caught wind?"

"I ain't the Pentagon neither, but I know when to keep my trap shut, and don't ask no questions I don't need to hear the answers to." He chewed two seconds in silence. "Edna helps out some-times at the hangar. She can't hear herself fart. You can rupture your throat just talking with her about the weather. I don't guess an eavesdropper would go away without an earful of something; but it's just talk. Even the damn government needs more'n that to make a stink."

Not a private citizen, though. All an interested fourth party would need is the rumor of cash about to change hands; but I didn't say that. It was definite: I liked Major Jack Flagg. Enough anyway not to put him wise, and consequently in the line of fire. He'd spent too much time flying solo. He would talk to himself just for the conversation; it didn't matter who else might be lis-tening.

TWENTY-TWO

urning off Conner, I slowed down as I pulled alongside the trailer Palm Volker used for an office; but Flagg told me to keep going. I knew where we were headed then.

Raw, rucked-up earth and a shred of yellow police tape remained alone as evidence of Clare Strickling's murder. The Piper Cub had been towed from where it had come to rest just short of the chain-link fence outside Golden Eagle Excursions. The hangar's bay door was raised. Inside, fluorescent tubes in overhead troughs spilled pale blue light down on the two ranks of aircraft facing each other across the aisle. Someone was moving around inside; a shadow flickered about with the restless animation of industry.

I parked in roughly the same spot as last time—yesterday, if you're going by the solar calendar. The world was turning faster than usual, skidding out from under my feet while I stood still. The green Suburban with the single taillight was no longer in its place where the airfield employees left their vehicles; one pigeon had yet to return to its coop. Flagg leapt out almost before we stopped moving, rheumatism be damned. He spat out his gum and took off toward the hangar, leaning forward from the hips like a chimpanzee, only less ungainly. Maybe it was something in the Juicy Fruit.

The building was shaped like a barrel cut in half and laid length-
wise, flat side down. We stepped into a woozy atmosphere of gasoline, diesel fuel, heavy motor oil, and stale exhaust, along with
something far more acrid, like acetate or pitch, some close cousin
of the cement that comes with a hobby kit. To our right, between
the skeletal helicopter and the fiberglass shell of a wingless glider,
sat a top-wing single-engine plane minus its propeller and nose section. It had the look of a large friendly hog. No one would mistake it
for a murder weapon. Across from it, in a cleared space big enough
to contain three aircraft, stood a ship barely half the Cub's size,
with stacked wings and a skin of canvas or some synthetic fabric;
some of this had been peeled away from the wooden frame and
hung in a loose triangle halfway back to the paddle-shaped tail.
A three-foot section of the exposed pine was a brighter color than
the rest, almost yellow; here a faint sawmill scent groped its way
through the chemical fumes. Kindling lay in a pile on the cement
floor, punctured with wormholes and stained the spongy brackish
black of dry rot.

There was something shameful about my presence there, as if
I'd walked in on a dainty creature only half-dressed.

Palm Volker leaned halfway out from a stepladder near the
front of the machine, a broad square plasterer's brush in one hand,
smearing ocher-colored goop onto the stretched fabric from a
five-gallon bucket balanced on the ladder's platform. This was
the source of that sharp, olfactory-eroding stench. Her rich brown
hair was tied up in a paisley-print bandanna. She had on canvas gloves, an olive-green tank top soaked through with sweat,
khaki cargo shorts that came to mid-thigh, and bulbous-toed Red
Wings, all striped and spattered with glistening viscous stuff
from the bucket. Concealing those tanned legs in jodhpurs ought
to have violated a city ordinance of some kind.

She grinned down at us over her shoulder. "I'd tell you to grab a brush, but there's an art to it; you can't spread it too thick or too thin."

"You ain't telling me nothing I don't know," Flagg said, as if she'd been talking to him. "You forget who sold you that kite?"

"I haven't bought it yet. You said you'd cut me a break if I made all the repairs."

"Did I? You can't hold an old man to any promises he forgot." He stripped the foil off a fresh stick of gum, winking at me. "She don't look much like no movie star, does she?" He meant the biplane. "Not much she don't. She just stole the show from Clara Bow, Errol Flynn, Jean Harlow, and that fresh kid, Leonardo Di-whatzisname."

Palm dipped her brush and scraped it on the rim of the bucket. "*Wings, Hell's Angels,* both *Dawn Patrols,* and *The Aviator.*" She sang the titles. "And all that's *after* it drove the Germans all the way back to Berlin in 1918."

"The Sopwith Snipe," I said. "Someone showed me a picture once, can't think who."

But she was talking to the plane now and didn't hear. "I've got feelers out to the Yankee Air Museum at Willow Run; going to take part in the air show next spring and pay off the mortgage on the field. That's if I get to keep her. Jack's going to coach me but, honestly, this thing can fly itself. The pilot's just the passenger."

"Keep telling yourself that, sweetie," Flagg said. "That model killed more Yanks than the Spanish flu. It's a bronco, not a show horse. The minute it figures out you don't belong in the saddle, boy howdy! Run you straight into the ground."

"Don't try to talk me out of it, old-timer. How many hours does this Bentley have left, by the way?" She rapped the side of the nose with the end of her brush handle. It rang like a cathedral bell.

"Been six hundred since its last overhaul; only had a few thousand on it then. The fighting ended before it could get a real workout. The rest of it went into training and winning the war all over again in Hollywood. Put that back!" he yelled. "That dope goes up on a hot date."

I'd thumped a cigarette out of the pack. I returned it. "Sorry. I got so caught up in the shoptalk. I see now why you brought me all the way out here in the middle of a murder investigation."

"Don't pretend you're bored by a little history," Palm said. "I've seen the car you drive." She balanced the brush on the edge of the bucket and climbed down. The long muscles in her thighs tensed and slackened. She shucked the gloves, snatched off the bandanna, and shook her hair loose. It tumbled to her shoulders like Tahquamenon Falls. "I can show off the plane anytime. It was just an excuse to get you both here. Jack has an interest in the conversation; his inventory was damaged and his workspace violated. But since his wife answered the phone I wasn't sure she'd approve. I wasn't sure she could hear me anyway."

"Don't you worry about Edna," he said. "She fell—"

"Two hundred feet onto a cement factory," Palm finished. "That drop gets steeper every time you tell it. She can't survive much more. You know she's more worried about you than she is about herself. If she found out we were talking about what happened downtown, it might make her mad enough to scotch the Snipe sale."

I said, "It's not definite Parrish's killing has anything to do with Strickling's. It shouldn't affect the airfield."

"Tell that to the FAA," she said. "Two deaths by unnatural causes, both involving Golden Eagle, my first and oldest client; one by way of a plane in my backyard. The investigation could drag on for a year, and what are the chances City Airport will stay interested in a partnership offer that long? They'll just wait till I default on the loan and snap the property up cheap." She smacked an unsmeared section of fuselage with the flat of her hand; the thump reverberated. "I may be barnstorming county fairs and high school football games for my supper till I'm Jack's age."

"What's so bad about that?" he said. "I'd still be doing it myself if I could get insurance."

My cell rang: I recognized the number. Listening, I retreated to the entrance. My part of the exchange consisted of the same word twice; and that was just to show the connection was working.

I thumbed off, looking around outside. Lunch was in progress. A pair of construction workers sat on folding chairs, playing two-handed euchre on an oil drum surrounded by kibitzers in hard hats. The crew and its equipment didn't seem to have made much progress against the mounds of gravel and masticated asphalt pushed up along the edge of the property.

I turned back. "Any chance we could continue this discussion somewhere less public than Ford Field?"

Palm pouted; but we left her project.

We walked the quarter-mile to the trailer, Major Jack Flagg outdistancing us both with his lunging stride.

The office was unchanged except for a large-scale drawing of architect's elevations in blue pencil on newsprint covering the desk like a tablecloth; from the look of the plan, a two-story concourse would occupy the center of the airfield, with identical hangars large enough to accommodate twice as many private airlines as existed at present.

Emmett Yale's voice echoed in my skull. I said, "Pipe dream?"

She flushed, gathering the plan into rough folds. "Not even that. No one's supposed to see this until we've got the thumbs-up from City Airport. I'm the practical partner; it's my job to turn my darling ex's delusions of grandeur into a fiscal reality." She stuffed the mass of paper into the deep drawer of the desk. "Okay, you've seen what I've got. Show me yours."

I glanced at Flagg studying the propeller on the wall. He

looked like he was trying to figure out how to straighten it. To all appearances that meant more to him than two murders connected with his livelihood; but then I might have to reach eighty myself to be in a position to judge his order of priorities.

"Where's your man Càndido?" I asked Palm. "I got the impression last time he did most of the chores around this place."

"It's his day off. I didn't think you struck up a friendship."

"We got close the last day or two. That was Inspector Alderdyce just now. He followed up a lead I gave him just before you sent for me. I guess this is one of those cases of the cobbler whose kids go barefoot. A man responsible for maintaining a busy place like an airfield ought to pay closer attention to the safety equipment on his own automobile. He got a ticket for a missing taillight assembly just outside Golden Eagle an hour before Gabe Parrish turned up dead in the Major's office."

TWENTY-THREE

Outside, a diesel engine started up with a concussive snort, shaking the trailer on its blocks; the lunch break was over. That ended the conference at that location. Communicating by signs, we went out and retraced our steps to the hangar and my car waiting outside.

Rolling away from the plosive racket, Palm in the front passenger's seat directed me to a place on Gratiot, five minutes away. As I made the turn onto the avenue I caught a glimpse in the mirror of Major Jack in the back seat; he'd traded his non-committal expression for a long pull of worry. He stared at the scenery without visible interest, the muscles of his jaw working at his gum as if that were the most important item on his list.

The building was a pole-barn affair with sheet-iron walls, standing on a plot adjoining the field along its southeast edge. A pedestal supported a decommissioned fighter jet out front, a cigarette-shaped fuselage with triangular wings. Tall white-tile letters running the length of the hip roof told us we'd arrived at THE WINDSOCK LOUNGE.

"It's a former VFW post," Palm said. "Jack was its last commander."

He made a noise between a grunt and a snarl. "Membership

kept dying off. Couldn't get new recruits after we stopped winning wars."

"The new owners got the idea for the gimmick when they inherited the jet. The plan was to sell the place to the airport, make money off the passengers waiting for their flight, but City turned it down. That was a mistake. I want to take the place over. That's when and if we come to an arrangement on annexation."

It seemed to me she was rolling the dice without stopping to see if she'd made the point last time; but high-finance and Heisenberg's principle were all the same to me. I kept my mouth shut.

A hostess in a pillbox hat, bolero jacket, and a pencil skirt conducted us to the booth Palm requested, in a corner equidistant from the more populated area on the other side of the circular bar and the jukebox pounding the Fifth Dimension playbook over the speakers.

"I'll junk the Pan Am hoke," Palm murmured under the beat, "change the name, the works. The jet set's ancient history. Airline passengers don't want to be reminded they're about to pack themselves into a tin can for x amount of hours with a bunch of Amazons calling the shots. It's probably what blew the deal in the first place."

Our waitress looked less comfortable in her uniform, which was designed for a smaller woman, but she managed the same square smile. None of us was hungry enough to invite excessive interruption, so we ordered from the drinks menu. Everything was named after a type of combat aircraft. Palm asked for a Spitfire—gin with bitters and a hot-pepper garnish—I unscrambled the "Russian MiG" to mean a vodka martini. Flagg, after tugging at his loose lower lip and staring at nothing, looked up. "Do I gotta call it P-51 Piss to get a beer?"

The square smile flickered, came back. "Bottled or draft?"

"It all comes from the same horse, don't it?"

She carried away the menus.

Palm looked at him. "What's the matter with you?"

"I got other things to think about than how to order a Bud Lite."

She switched her attention to me. "What you said doesn't make sense. Càndido's an acquired taste, but he's serious about his work. He wouldn't be the first maintenance man to be careless when it comes to his own car, but he's no killer."

"Not this side of the border anyways," said Flagg.

I looked at him this time; but Palm spoke up before I could pump him.

"He came asking for work last year. He had his green card and I was short-handed, so I took a chance on a stranger without references. I've never had reason to regret it. He's a one-man crew."

Our drinks came. Flagg snatched his mug off the tray while the waitress was lowering it. After she left I asked him how the man had gotten under his skin.

"Jack thinks every foreigner is a spy."

I looked at Palm. "Amazing. His lips didn't even move."

Flagg said, "I been burned before. I hired a migrant for my ground crew in Bisbee back in '72, when all the talent was in the military. He had that same homemade tattoo on his wrist. I caught him nicking the fuel line on my Beechcraft and turned him over to the law. He spilled. See, he worked for the Colombians, so it was a shock when he found out it's harder to wriggle out of a jam up here. They hired him to set up a trade route: I was to start shipping junk in my return flights from over the border if I wanted to keep my planes in the air. Crashing one with four people aboard was supposed to get my attention."

"Càndido's never tried to shake me down," Palm said; "not even for a raise. You can't hang a man because he tattoos his arm and speaks broken English."

I said, "It wouldn't make any difference if he wore a tie and talked like Prince Charles. He followed me all the way to my client's place of business and then again almost back to my office.

By then he knew where I was going, so he broke off. He didn't tail me here. The cops haven't had time to track him down based on that ticket, but he might have figured out I'd spotted him and got spooked. There's a BOLO out on his heap, for what it's worth. With that head start he could be halfway to Toronto in a hot Toyota."

She stirred her swizzle around her glass. She hadn't drank from it yet. "What possible reason could he have for killing this man Parrish?"

"The Major was negotiating a fare to fly Clare Strickling to Canada; there's no law against that, if you don't ask too many questions. The way it works out, Càndido overheard Jack discussing the deal with his hard-of-hearing wife and decided to cut himself in, but since he couldn't be expected to do any flying, he arranged to meet Strickling to collect payment as a go-between, planning to kill him as soon as he was sure he had the cash on him, dead men being preferable to dissatisfied customers. That was supposed to happen in Strickling's apartment, but plans changed when I stumbled in and the mark got antsy and changed the location to the Golden Eagle hangar. That wasn't a problem, though, because an airplane propeller's as good as a gun if you've worked around an airfield long enough to learn a few things. Disabling the security cameras was one. He could do that and blame it on the construction crew; it had happened often enough even they couldn't deny it.

"All very tidy; except I wasn't part of the deal, and got the money first." I looked at them both. "That's new information. Even the cops don't know that part. Càndido saw me pick it up; had to, or he'd have got it himself. He couldn't fight me for it and make me a witness who could identify him, and he couldn't kill me out there in the open even if he had another airplane in his pocket for backup. So he decided to shadow me, hoping I'd lead him to it."

She'd stopped stirring. "So much for Strickling—if you're not just spinning a yarn. Why Parrish?"

"That was my fault; I've dealt with blackmailers before, and should have known by things he said in Flagg's office that he'd seen the murderer in the act and was looking for a payoff. I surprised him in Flagg's office. He was expecting Càndido. They had an appointment."

Flagg set down his mug and used a gnarled knuckle to whisk foam from his upper lip. "But if he knew the Mex didn't get the money—" He stopped. "Sure. It's dark in that hangar. You can't see a damn thing looking out into bright daylight."

I nodded. "Being hidden inside—which of course Parrish denied he was, not wanting to cut me in on what he knew—he'd have seen who started up that plane and set it rolling, but not me standing outside. The sun was reflecting so bright off the cabin windows I couldn't tell if anyone was in it. It would've been in his eyes. He didn't see me pick up the money. That's what he was after in return for keeping his mouth shut."

Palm drank then, using her thumb to hold the swizzle out of the way like a spoon in a coffee cup. She swallowed and put the glass down half-empty; shook her head. "I don't buy it."

Neither did I, now that I'd heard it from my own lips. It fell short in one important particular. But I didn't say anything. You don't attract business by admitting your mistakes.

TWENTY-FOUR

She made up for lost time; when I looked again, her glass was empty. "This morning I had only one murder to worry about," she said; "now it's two, plus a direct connection to the first by way of an employee of this airfield. Remind me not to ask you for any more updates."

I said, "It might not be as bad as all that. Look at Northwest: the unsolved strangulation of a stewardess, a planeload of dead passengers, and a plot to cut the lone survivor out of a settlement; all that against it, and it took simple bureaucratic incompetence to drive the company into receivership. Even then the suits all bailed out with golden parachutes—which as metaphors go is almost moronically ironic."

"Northwest could afford to drag its feet. I can't. The feds can knock me out of the air and not have to worry I'll come back at them with an army of lawyers." She reached across the table to touch my hand. "What'll it cost to hire you to make this go away?"

I hated to do it; not because I needed another client, but because her fingers felt so smooth and warm on the back of my hand. I disengaged myself and patted hers. "Your money's no good. I'm still with the original firm. All I have to do is deliver an ironclad double-murderer and I can retire until the next pushover job comes my way."

Major Jack made that noise like a punctured blimp: the one that meant he was amused. He signaled the waitress for another round.

"This one's on me. I duked it out with Chairman Mao, ran medical supplies to Haiti, and had my last rites read to me in a burn unit in Frisco, but this is my first homicide case. Let those sonsabitches in New York say my memoirs ain't commercial now."

"I'll take a raincheck." I had a text from Alderdyce. He'd had Càndido brought in for questioning.

There was a time factor involved, so I asked Palm if she'd take Flagg back to his office. She shook her head.

"All I've got is the bike. I traded my Toyota for it to save on mileage; that's how tight my budget is since I took on the airfield."

Flagg said, "I ain't brittle. I can ride on the handlebars if you don't want me copping a feel from behind."

"Operating a motorcycle in Detroit is hairy enough without a passenger along to break my concentration. I won't take the chance of destroying a national treasure."

I got up, cutting the Major off in mid-sneer. Too many years had passed since he'd ridden the edge for him to appreciate the situation. Caution isn't fear. It's a response conditioned by experience.

"I'll buy that round later." I laid cash on the table. "This one's on the client. The Healy Building's on my way. I'll drop you off."

He unslung his bomber jacket from the back of his chair, sliding his arms into the sleeves in that overhead gesture I could never manage. "Kids. Think dying of old age is a good thing."

I found Alderdyce drinking water from a flimsy plastic bottle in front of the same window I'd sat behind last time, looking at myself in the trick mirror. He'd put on an autumn-weight brown suit and a yellow necktie with one of the shirts he had made special to accommodate the planes and angles of his torso. On the other side of the glass Càndido gazed without expression at the black detective sergeant I'd met before, sitting across from him polishing his glittering gold-rimmed eyeglasses with a special cloth. The plainclothesman looked less crisp today, in his shirtsleeves with damp circles under the arms. The suspect by contrast sat as immobile as a hood ornament.

"They're born that way," the inspector said, "our brothers south of the border. Either that, or they rented *Wrestling Women versus the Aztec Mummy* too many times. You could strike a match off their conscience."

"Uncooperative, I'm guessing."

"Worse. He knows he'll be out of here in time for siesta. Liberation, mi amigo; she's on her way."

He was running out of xenophobic slurs, I could tell. I broke his rhythm.

"Lawyer?"

"No. Well, he probably is; but try throwing a brick anywhere in the District without hitting a mouthpiece of some kind. This isn't your garden-variety shyster, with a habeas on his corpus. Our guest used his phone call to reach the State Department. Had the card in his wallet, with an extension number and everything." He crushed the bottle between two fingers. "Next time you throw me a person of interest, make sure he hasn't swung an asylum deal with Uncle Sam."

"Colombians?" Flagg's saboteur in Arizona had put the idea in my brain.

"Mexican Mafia. He's a dead duck if he goes back to Zacatecas. State's got too much invested in what he gave them to let him face deportation for a crummy little misdemeanor like Murder One."

"Get anything out of him at all?"

"Not even his real name; that's government property, like the bill for his relocation here. Our tax dollars at work. They even pressured the chief to make that moving violation go away. I wonder what laws I'd have to bust to land a sweet deal like that."

"Is that all you had on him?"

"If he croaked Parrish, he didn't have the courtesy to leave behind a skin cell, let alone fingerprints. But show me even one perp who didn't watch *CSI* and take notes."

"Does he need a ride to the impound?"

"You moonlighting for Uber now?"

"My car's too old for that. Some people like to make conversation, especially when it's a civilian breaking the ice. I don't have to cooperate with Washington."

"If there were more Clark Kents like you around, this here mighty engine of justice could go part-time. I'm guessing he's already got a ride. We picked him up in a garage on Dix, where he was getting that taillight fixed. Ernie's; except it's changed management a couple of times since Ernie Bunch went to the can for fencing discontinued test cars without telling Chrysler. State won't let its barefoot boy out of its sight on the way, in case we try to bust him for littering or setting a homeless family on fire. Whatever he gave them must have been worth the investment."

"I know Ernie's. Toss his car?"

He showed his teeth. "Naw. We thought we'd wait for the grease monkeys to do that and call us when they found a nine-millimeter pistol under the driver's seat with a round missing. Get the fuck out of here."

I did as directed; but I'd barely been listening. The idea that had come my way needed twice the concentration just to make it half-baked.

There wasn't a legal space in front of the precinct, but my car was still there when I came out. The two or three blocks surrounding an official building are a kind of demilitarized zone, and anyway the cops who work Homicide don't go around sticking tickets under windshields. I sat behind the wheel, twisting the radio dial and watching the shifts change. On WJR we were enjoying unseasonably warm weather, with no precipitation in sight. On WWJ high winds were coming our way up the East Coast, bringing along a taste of early November in the way of sleet and freezing rain. Both stations claimed the same source.

I switched off just as a maroon Lincoln Navigator boated up to the curb just in front of me. The driver got out, stretched the Friendly Skies out of his bones, and crossed the sidewalk, wearing one of the black Polyester suits the government bought at the last Kmart bankruptcy sale. He was a pudgy thirty with curly orange hair retreating from a forehead spackled heroically with freckles; it looked like the splash pattern in a forensics photo. Maybe that's how he'd happened to draw this particular detail.

I turned the radio back on. The meteorologist on WJR had caught up with the storm forecast, speaking as if that's what he'd been saying right along. By then the car was rocking on its springs with ice crystals strafing the windows at an angle parallel to the street. Frost fogged the windshield. I switched the heater to full blast. The blower came on with a smell of parched metal and scorched dust and the glass cleared. If this kept up, all the little pirates and Harry Potters were going to have to wear thermals under their costumes come October.

Beltway Bill came out ten minutes later, accompanied by Càndido. The maintenance man had changed coveralls, but they'd begun to collect a fresh set of stains and in a day or two would be indistinguishable from the others. His first action at the top of the steps was to ruck back both sleeves, exposing the prison tattoo on his left wrist; he'd have covered it from instinct alone when he was pinched, as if that was all that marked him as a crook in police eyes. The State Department man didn't handle him like a felon; that was to be expected from a desk jockey, but it wouldn't have been in his orders to open the car door for him, yet he did that. This was probably his first trip outside his cubicle.

Not that the courtesy brought any sunlight into Càndido's expression. I'd seen happier-looking parties going into police stations wearing cuffs instead of coming out unfettered. But then he'd never looked like one of those laughing bandits in old westerns. He was probably part Indian, a class that hadn't much to smile about since Cortez.

I gave them a block before I pulled out behind. I knew where they were going; I just wanted to get there before the sourpuss ward of the government got back behind the wheel of his own car.

On Dix a crumbling asphalt drive led up a hill to a grubby brick building that might have been home to every repair shop in automobile history, right down to the inert gas blazing bright orange through a tube twisted like a balloon animal to read ERNIE'S AUTO CLINIC. We climbed past mud-clad cars and pickups waiting their turns at one of the two repair bays. Letters stenciled on the pull-up doors said HONK FOR SERVICE. A black lockbox was bolted next to the blank narrow fire door marked OFFICE, with a sign directing latecomers to drop their keys into the slot after hours and leave their vehicles overnight.

The Navigator parked a few slots down from where I'd put in. An altercation of some kind broke out when the State man alighted along with his passenger; the wind was stiffening, hurling projectiles from Pennsylvania, and the words were snatched away before they reached me. Finally the Mexican made a casting-away gesture with one arm and stalked toward the entrance with his nanny scrambling to catch up on his chubby legs. Càndido must have given Justice another El Chapo to rate all that attention.

I was catching up on the weather reports when one of the bay doors slid up and a familiar-looking SUV rolled out of the garage, with an even more familiar-looking face behind the windshield. It didn't look any happier than it had before; in fact, circumstances seemed to have gotten worse. His mouth was working, and what was coming out of it with no one to hear it ought to have melted a hole through the glass. Maybe he didn't like the size of the repair bill. The bureaucrat in the double-knit suit stood inside the bay with his hands in his pockets.

He didn't move until the green Suburban swung into the street, its brand-new taillight assembly looking chipper across from its dusty mate. Then he went back to the Navigator, pulled out into the drive, and turned at the end, heading in the opposite direction. His assignment was finished.

It wasn't the bill that had put Càndido out of sorts, even if the taxpayers weren't paying it; it was that gray eminence from Washington breathing down his neck. I spun the wheel, let both parties go their separate ways, and got out of the car, using both hands to push the door open against the gust that tried to slam it in my face.

TWENTY-FIVE

The office had come off the same assembly line as all the others, just like the automobiles it serviced: a little larger than a gas station restroom, tiled similarly, with a faux-wainscot counter that came to the sternum, a couple of molded plastic chairs to seat the customers waiting for their oil changes and tire rotations, a side door leading into the garage, and a rack of extended-warranty pamphlets that covered a replacement cigar lighter if you were rear-ended by a 1946 Hudson in a blizzard in Tahiti. The kid behind the counter came with the package: head shaved all around, leaving a topknot of greasy brown hair shaped like a birthday cake, features crowded into the middle of a narrow pale pustuled face, and a label on his blue work shirt that said his name was D'Andre; but I wasn't buying it. He looked more like a Brad to me.

"D'Andre didn't make it in today, I guess," I said. "You'd think a ritzy place like this could afford more than one shirt per employee."

I gave up waiting for that to register on his screen and showed him the county star. From the looks of him the stage prop would be just his speed. "Customer you just served. Did you wait on him when he dropped off his car?"

He worked on that, picking his nose in his mind. "You police?"

I put it back in my pocket. I didn't have the time while he learned to read. "We got all the answers you need back at head-quarters. You got all the answers I want right here. Which is it?"

"Yeah, that was him." His expression didn't change. It might not have been capable of it. His brain needed all the energy avail-able to fill and empty his lungs.

"What'd he give you then that he couldn't collect today in front of his buddy in the black suit?"

"Huh?"

I downshifted into low, spacing out the words.

"The gun, Hawking. The cops didn't find it in his car, and he couldn't reclaim it in front of his babysitter. Open the till."

"Are you robbing the place?"

He was stalling. He had brains enough for that.

"Does it matter?" I slid a thumb inside my jacket. The Chief's Special was thirty feet away in my glove compartment.

Understanding came into his face like thick pea soup coming to a boil. I knew then I wouldn't find what I wanted in the drawer; but once you start a thing you have to see it through or they won't be so easy next time. I hoped to hell there wouldn't be a next time; wit as dim as his can be septic.

He pressed a key on the cash register. I lunged across the counter and had a grip on his wrist before the drawer finished sliding open. I wasn't disappointed. The bills and checks lay flat inside, next to a brass key with a round tab. No room in there for ord-nance. I let go. I had a sudden inspiration.

"What about the lockbox?"

"Lockbox?"

He was stalling. I started to get excited; no one is that consis-tently stupid. This one wouldn't have the stamina to stick it out. "Outside." I pointed at the key.

His pimples vanished in the rush of blood to his face. "There's nothing in it. That's for after closing."

"It's my time to waste. Don't worry; it's not your gratuity I'm after. Just the key." I waggled my fingers.

"I should call the manager."

"Knock yourself out. Key first."

I snatched it from his hand and went outside. Behind me I heard another door slam shut: That would be the exit through the garage. You didn't have to be the brightest animal in the forest to appreciate the principle of fight-or-flight. Entry-level laborers like him could always find another minimum-wage job in the current market; their prospects were better there than in stir.

The black box attached to the door fastened with a hinged lid, slotted to receive a work order and an ignition key. A single turn released the lock and the box released a no-nonsense piece into my hand: a Beretta U.S. M9 semi-automatic, chambered for the nine-millimeter Parabellum round. D'Andre-slash-Brad was careful, for all his evolutionary shortcomings: Waiting for his customer to reclaim the weapon he'd stashed before the cops showed up, he'd have shunted it between a temporary haven like the cash drawer and the outside box while the garage was open for business and it had been emptied of its overnight cargo.

I wanted to kick out the magazine, see if it was missing a cartridge, but just holding the pistol with a handkerchief wrapped around my hand was awkward enough. The cops could do that. They had more experience in handling murder weapons without smudging the prints, if D'Andre *du jour* hadn't already done that. I dropped the key into the box and scuttled to the car with my prize pinned under my arm, turning my other shoulder into the wind, anxious to protect the surface evidence from the sleet but careful not to grip it too tightly and wipe out what remained. I was like a young mother holding her first baby.

John Alderdyce had a lot to learn about expressing gratitude. He peeled away the covers from the item I'd deposited on his desk and glared at it as if it were a smoldering sack of excrement.

"How long have you been sitting on this little egg?"

"Twenty minutes, driving white-knuckle. Visibility's zero." I told him how I'd come by it.

"Chain of possession," he said. "Due process. Search and seizure. Inadmissible evidence. Stop me when I come to something you've heard about."

I grinned. "You had me at 'Chain of possession.' You know that sexy lawyer talk makes me go all squishy inside."

"You think you can make this go away with smart yap?"

"Okay, here's the chain: Càndido to D'Andre to me. Tinker to Evers to Chance. Ernie's record is bad enough without accessory to murder; in a way, that makes the place more useful than a legit business. They'll have the clerk's real name, address, and Social Security number on file, so he can be brought in and promised immunity for turning the Mexican. Then there's the work order on his car and the copy of the receipt with Càndido's signature on it. With all that, fingerprints are practically an afterthought."

"The defense will give you an argument there; only they won't have to, even if there's a single liftable print anywhere on it, *because* the prosecution won't take it into court, *because* any judge in the system would throw the gun out, *because* it was obtained without a warrant."

"I've got the Michigan Penal Code on audio: Civilians don't need any paperwork, and I just gave you chain-of-possession for dummies. Also the clerk gave it up voluntarily. The key, that is."

"All without you bouncing him off the floor or—oh, say, impersonating a police officer."

"Let's skip the details and focus on the big picture."

He lifted the pistol in the handkerchief and studied it. Then he rewrapped it carefully—his big, blocked-out hands with their thick fingers were as delicate as a surgeon's—and returned it to the desk. "Guns are notoriously unreliable when it comes to prints. We might get a partial off the magazine or a shell. It's the right caliber; if the ballistics check out and this is the gun that killed Parrish, we might ease it past the county prosecutor. She's a good sport, and more than half cop."

"I'd move fast," I said. "While the cypher from State's still in the air with his phone turned off. By the time he gets a return flight, you may be able to sweat a confession out of his boy."

"Stop being so irritatingly pessimistic and wait outside. You're way past due for a formal statement." He put down the gun and picked up his telephone.

I stopped at the coffee station in the common room, tossed a handful of coins onto the tray, and poured department turpentine into my empty stomach. I had too much respect for him to duck out until I'd emptied the cup.

There was no reason not to hang around and give him what he wanted. I couldn't move forward until the slow steady machinery of justice turned up something on the latest crumb of evidence and pulled in the once-and-future suspect for another war of wills downtown in the little room with the Judas window; but if *I* were a fugitive from La Salsa Nostra and my cover had been blown once already, I'd have put at least two states between myself and the Second Precinct already. After all, I had a brand-new taillight burning a hole in my pocket. My part of the paperwork could wait.

The Strickling part of the case still needed adjustment. The money motive is flexible; it can be twisted into an endless variety of shapes to fit any investigation. Often the amount doesn't matter. A bottle-deposit slip could be reason enough to crack someone's skull with a monkey wrench, but an airplane propeller is not a monkey wrench. Twenty thousand, even in untraceable cash, was small coin in return for the prospect of life in a cage. Depending upon his place in the organization, Càndido would be accustomed to handling bales of the stuff, and even if none of it stuck to his fingers, just suspecting there was so much more of it around made chump change of anything that fit inside an office portfolio.

He *might* chance it, being an exile in a strange country; but it was unlikely. For sure, Gabe Parrish, Yale's security chief, wouldn't bend down to pick it up. Six-figure jobs don't come along often, especially when you've been canned by Yale for blackmail.

Not for twenty thousand. Not for ten times that. I wondered just how much a speculator like Strickling could make off a trade on Wall Street; Yale had said seven figures, but that was a guess. Of course it would depend on how much Strickling risked; but risk didn't loom so large when you had a sure thing like a tip that your boss intends to channel millions into the same deal.

Barry Stackpole, my faithful on-ramp to the Information Superhighway, could give me a fair idea of how much I was dealing with. He'd run a modest career in exposing the crimes of the mighty into an enterprise that had attracted the wary attention of national security. Unwind something as simple as stock manipulation. I needed a landline to pump him, preferably analog enough to foil today's long-distance tapping technology. The wires leading to my Edwardian pile on Grand River hadn't been replaced since before the Bay of Pigs.

So I got back on my plastic horse and followed the groove back to the office. In the last block I passed the usual line of cars standing against the curb, unobtrusive models belonging to the day-laborers and file clerks who worked in the neighborhood. The scenery never changed, apart from the order in which the vehicles were parked. That made it easy to spot the lime-green Suburban sporting its bright new taillight assembly just down from the front door of my building.

TWENTY-SIX

The sleet had stopped, but the windows of the SUV were streaked with melting ice crystals, so I couldn't tell if anyone was inside, and I didn't want to linger. I took the corner at cruising speed, left the car in the usual spot, and walked back around to the front door, not paying any particular attention to my surroundings; I might even have whistled if I could work up the saliva. The Chief's Special was a snug weight on my lumbar region.

The foyer contained the daily odors of Pine-Sol, generic furniture wax, and Rosecranz's answer to authentic Borodino borscht, with an aftertaste of worm-eaten wood from old-growth white pine, the degenerating skeleton of the building. The smell of danger stood no chance against the fug of an old building.

If it had any smell at all. It seemed to me I'd have noticed it sometime or other.

I climbed the stairs with the unselfconscious gait of a bit player trying to walk across a stage without tripping on his lines. The .38 was in my hand. I draw it in my sleep, like Wild Bill.

I gave myself a pep talk: He didn't have his gun, that was safe in police custody. I argued for the other side: It's Detroit, Pollyanna; you can get one when you turn in your tickets at Chuck E. Cheese. I told myself to shut up and started up the second flight.

No use trying to be quiet; each tread had its own sour note, like an out-of-tune piano. I pressed my back against the wall and slid up along the warped plaster, towed by the gun. If he was waiting on the landing to pick me off, he'd be lying on the floor on his side, counting on me to look higher up for his head and arm when they showed past the corner. Then again, maybe not. An amateur would try for a standing-up shot; so would a professional counting on another professional to expect him to act professional. Cops-and-robbers is a shell game: If a bullet doesn't put you on the ground, the convoluted logic will send you to the psych ward.

I pushed the envelope; damn near tore right through it. I took the last three steps in a bound, spun on my heel, and threw down on the hallway that ran past my office. The pea-green walls, ribbed rubber floor runner, and schoolhouse bowl fixtures stared at me without blinking. I got that foolish feeling a tree gets when it falls in the forest and there's no one to hear it.

Now I had to do it all over again.

At my door I hugged the wall, gun arm across my chest, reached across and turned the knob with my free hand. When no bullets shattered the pebbled glass I flung the door inward and pirouetted to stand in the doorway in the approved commando manner, feet spread, left hand gripping right wrist, the revolver trained at chest level.

The waiting room was empty. The private door across from me was ajar. I changed the lock more often than the batteries in the smoke detector, but in my work it's a legitimate tax deduction.

I was fed up. I threw away the manual and went in the way I did normally, except for the weapon in my hand, hip-high now.

It's always the small details that catch my eye: the striated hole punched through the window behind my desk, the grubby canvas tool bag sprawled open on the floor, the door of my safe hanging open slightly crooked, like a broken jaw. Only a trained observer like me would save the dead Mexican for last.

He looked as if he'd died in mid-prayer, the ultimate state of grace. He was on his knees in front of the safe, and only the door, wrenched half off its hinges by his pry bar, had prevented him from falling over onto his side. His shoulder leaned against it, his head cocked backward, eyes fixed on the ceiling and his mouth hanging open, frozen in the act of gasping or screaming; the concept of instantaneous death can't be proven or disproven until someone comes back from the grave to report.

It would have been plenty quick, though. The bullet had entered his chest almost under the arm and must have passed through both lungs into his heart; the blood slicking the right side of his torso had stopped flowing before it could drip on the floor. His left arm was raised, the hand gripping the safe's top shelf as if to hang on to what life was left in him. The sleeve of his coveralls had slid down to the elbow, exposing the DIY tattoo on his wrist, a gang sign of some kind, possibly cribbed from a Mayan tomb, or more appropriately a place of human sacrifice. He might have stepped down from one of those walls himself; even in death his face was all bunched flesh, like an infant possessed by a demon. The shelf he was grasping was where I'd stashed the banded bills from Clare Strickling's portfolio. The stacks were intact. Càndido hadn't had time to count them and figure out the size of the estate he was leaving.

I left the corpse unfrisked. The taxpayers weren't paying me for that. There was nothing of interest in his bag, just the usual jumble of industrial-grade hand- and power tools, the wrenches bent and twisted to accommodate their specific uses.

The hole in the window was almost a perfect circle, punctured at high velocity; damp air whistled through it. I approached it on tiptoe, as if Natty Bumppo had made it and was aiming to put another round through the same hole. Something bumped the sill when I braced myself against it; I was still holding the .38. I holstered it and put my eye to the hole. It lined up directly with the roof of the empty building across the street, the place where I'd parked my car through all its changes of management and bankruptcies. There was no sign of Natty or anyone else. I picked up the phone. The first number on your speed dial says a lot about you. Mine's Homicide.

TWENTY-SEVEN

The usual alluvium of strangers had accumulated in the hallway, craning for a look at the chorus line of detectives, uniforms, morgue attendants, photographers, print experts, and forensic specialists carrying their poker faces in and out of my two hundred square feet of business practice, like visitors to a cramped stateroom in a Marx Brothers gag. They were my office neighbors, but the cast kept changing, and even the veterans were just part of the scenery, like the Wilson-era wiring and lead-based paint on the walls; we hadn't made enough of an impression to exchange names, let alone Christmas cards. Before the body-bag boys gathered up their load, a horse-faced detective third-grade whose flattop haircut made him look at least thirty stretched a measuring tape from the hole in the window to the hole in the corpse, reeled it in with a snap, and declared that the shot had been fired from the roof of the two-story hulk across the street. I let him have the scoop; I hadn't used a precision instrument.

When the bag and its contents disappeared down the stairs the crowd dwindled to just us three: John Alderdyce, the young plain-clothesman from the Second with the glittering eyeglassware, and me. The place seemed emptier than usual after all that.

Alderdyce looked down at the stacks of bills now on the desk, fists in his pockets as if someone might accuse him of skimming;

the amount had already been recorded in a squad-car officer's pad.

"I'm surprised you didn't stick it in a money market account," the inspector said. "I mean, as long as you were going to sit on the evidence, for as long as you were going to sit on it. Draw some interest to help you sleep nights in the joint."

I said, "I wasn't sure who it belonged to, the client or Strickling's estate or the SEC, to put toward the fines for insider trading. You wouldn't be much of a cop if I plunked down cash on a piece of German engineering and you didn't follow up on it, and I wouldn't be much of a criminal mastermind if I thought you wouldn't. Face it, John: We're trapped by our circumstances. Money just makes it worse. It sure has for me."

He switched subjects. After all those interrogations he could throw a changeup like Mickey Lolich. "What was Strickling carrying it in? I don't see you scooping this many cakes of currency off the ground while the looky-loos stood around with their hands in their pockets."

I bent down, plucked the torn transparent plastic bag from the wastebasket, and gave it to him. He didn't have to know about the portfolio yet. I suddenly had plans for it. I just didn't know what they were or why.

I said, "As far as he was concerned, everything was in place for him to fly out. He wouldn't know Càndido had cut himself in; maybe not even that he was just maintenance, and not an associate of Jack Flagg's. Just knowing about the arrangement gave him a leg up. I'd just about made up my mind to turn the cash over to you when I spotted the Suburban out front."

I hardly expected him to believe that. I wasn't sure I did, apart from not wanting anything to do with that kind of money. The more I learned in the course of an investigation the less I knew about myself.

Whether he bought it or not I'll never know, because he switched again.

"Well, this clears up two murders. Be nice if that'd happen without a third one landing in our lap. A guy can dream." He nodded at Gold Glasses, who shook open the bag and scooped the bills in through the hole. "See you back at the barn."

The detective, whose name was Gröstark, hugged the parcel to his chest. "Maybe."

I grinned at the door closing behind him. "No one told me he was funny."

"He isn't. Let's go see what the boys left us across the street. They don't overlook things; but the one time you don't check."

There's something about a failed retail business that's bleaker than an abandoned farmhouse, which at least has the panache of pathos; of a struggle to maintain hope, borne on a family's back for seasons on end, heartbreak at the finish, and sad broken furniture left behind. It's a failure of a different sort, without anything so glamorous as tragedy.

Just why a relatively well-built structure on a moderately well-traveled street should see so many bistros, beaneries, salons, storm-door emporia, health-food stores, video rentals, and medical marijuana dispensaries come and go while a seedy dump at the end of an industrial cul-de-sac should continue peddling the same overpriced junk for decades is a mystery that's always explained in hindsight, applying a theory that stands up only until the next enterprise collapses after having followed all the rules down to the letter. It was a double puzzle that I had watched the whole melancholy parade with the wolf snarling at my own door the whole time.

The building was an oblong of streaked yellow stucco with

glass-block windows and a sign on the front door advertising three thousand square feet of retail space with accommodations on the second floor for residential or office use. I'd never met the absentee landlord; but then the syndicate that cashed my own rent checks was a faceless body with a name you could knock out of a piñata blindfolded; based in China, in a city that by now could with justification call itself Detroit-on-the-Yangtze.

The sun had come out, drying the puddles left by the miniature ice storm, but the shadowy stretch behind the building hadn't gotten the news. A monster oil pig left over from the '73 energy crisis stood nearly as high as the roof, a great pitted canned-ham affair with a pipe ladder welded to it leading to the fill spout on top. The ladder was coated with ice, hobnailed with frozen droplets growing rotten in the slowly rising temperature, but still treacherous despite the tread of the crew that had scaled it minutes ago to investigate the source of the shot. It fell away in tube-shaped sheets when Alderdyce started to climb, tinkling like wind chimes when they struck the ground. His foot slipped once. He kept his grip, sparing me the impossibility of catching him but showering me with icy shards that found their way under my collar through sheer homing instinct. Could've been worse; I could've been pressed duck under two hundred ten pounds of city employee.

We stepped off the top of the tank onto the roof of the building. It was tar-covered, with a coating of gravel that crunched underfoot, accompanied by uneasy groans from the rafters supporting it. The wind had slowed to a steady fifteen miles per hour, but ten yards above the ground it felt like fifty. A wall three-and-a-half-feet high ran all around the edge, designed for no other possible purpose than to collect hundreds of gallons of rainwater to test the integrity of the construction. We crept to the opposite side and braced our hands on the top of the wall to look across the street.

I was racking up a lot of time lately looking over one wall or the other at a scene of grisly death.

I'd never seen my office from that angle. It had taken a bullet to remove a square inch of soot and pigeon filth from the glass. My desk and chair, wartime file cabinets, and *Custer's Last Stand* in its frame looked like the furnishings in a dollhouse. You wondered how the poor sap had stood the place thirty years.

A scatter of ice crystals had settled into the cracks in the mortar atop the wall. Alderdyce pointed at a bare spot where something had rested, possibly a rifle barrel; in a few minutes the melting would have removed even that faint trace. He straightened and stepped back, studying the roof at his feet. "Can't tell if he was standing or kneeling," he said. "Maybe the crew could, if they got here in time. That would give us a fair idea of the shooter's height, or lack of it."

I nodded. "That'd narrow it down; there being strict height regulations for membership in the International Brotherhood of Snipers."

"Constructive sarcasm is always welcome."

We climbed back down, taking our time even though most of the ice had melted; the rungs were still slick with moisture and not quite as cold as a sunken submarine. Back around in front of the deserted building, Alderdyce frowned at the Cutlass. "You weren't by chance considering a new paint job at least? That would leave eighteen grand for your retirement fund."

"You sound almost like you're sorry I can't keep the money."

"You can only see so much flowing back into the gaping gullet of insurance companies, fat cats, and the slush fund on Capitol Hill before you start wondering if what you do makes any difference at all."

"Probably doesn't. I know what: Call Detective Gröstark. If we catch him before he reports to the chief we won't have to split it four ways."

"Oh, go to hell." He stuck out his paw. It was like shaking hands with a train coupling.

Back in the dollhouse I broke out the broom and dustpan and cleared the little pile of pulverized glass from the floor: A sharp-shooter with a high enough powered rifle doesn't waste energy on collateral damage. I smoothed a piece of packing tape over the hole and left a message with Rosecranz to replace the pane; it was siesta time in Smolensk and his phone was off the hook. I pushed the safe door shut, gouging a semi-circle in the floor with its sagging corner. It didn't latch, of course, and it hung at a demented angle like a prizefighter's grin when the smelling salts brought him back around.

I pulled at my lower lip. Why a prizefighter? Gabe Parrish, of course; which led me back to Emmett Yale, and by the same mental train to Lloyd Lipton, Yale's dead stepson, and finally Clare Strickling, who may or may not have made his windfall from inside information provided by Lipton but probably hadn't sicced Melvin Weatherall onto the boss's stepson to shut him up; who nevertheless had come to his own untimely end by way of that miracle machine the automobile, designed to lead to freedom and luxury: Irony. The case dripped with it as much as it did with blood. And now Càndido's. Five degrees of separation, the Domino Effect, call it what you will; one man's death diminished all the rest.

I sat down, slid open the top drawer, and took out the cloth-and-faux-leather portfolio with its cargo of travel brochures: Strickling's Judas trail, to misdirect his pursuers while he took up a wealthy exile's residence somewhere else, Dubai, maybe, or Angmagssalik, which was too hard to pronounce to bother looking for him there. If twenty grand for a one-way flight was worth the layout, the stock deal must have made that look like matchsticks.

Inflation has the same impact on murder and blackmail as it has on ballpark franks. Even Càndido, petty crook that he may have been, seemed a stretch for the role of two-time killer, or for that matter a small-time burglary, over the amount of cash that had surfaced. But the bottom line would turn up with the rest of the money; when it turned up.

Where was it?

Suddenly the brochures didn't look so much like a diversion. If Strickling was planning to turn the cash over to Golden Eagle, why would he seal it up in plastic? It would have to be counted by the recipient. Opening a second package took time and added unnecessary anxiety to an already urgent situation. All he had to do was hand off the portfolio.

All of a sudden a common item of office supply had become as valuable as a stock-market killing.

I unzipped it, dumped the parti-colored pamphlets out onto the desk, and spread the file pockets again, just in case I'd missed something the first time—a scrap of notepaper, say, with a map to the buried loot, or a riddle written on a grain of rice.

Nothing. I flayed it wide on the desk. The sample business card showed through the little plastic window; no elves had come along to add anything to the Yale logo printed on it. I slid it out, turned it over, and looked at the ballpoint scribble on the back.

My first reaction wasn't triumph, or even satisfaction, but nausea. If I'd done that the first time around I might have saved two lives.

Or not. Maybe nothing you do makes any difference at all.

TWENTY-EIGHT

here didn't seem to be much point in putting the card in the safe, but I couldn't return it to its display pocket. Someone with a bigger brainpan than mine might find interest in a dummy with Yale's name on it and turn it over, or do so just by accident. Committing the information to memory wasn't beyond reach—it was only one line—but I had too much trouble just keeping track of my cell phone to trust my powers of retention, so destroying it was out.

I opened and shut some drawers, looked around me. Hiding something is harder than searching for it; all the best places are the first to strike the eye. Everyone knows about drawer bottoms, toilet tanks, and picture frames. From where I sat I could identify all the species of dead insects in the translucent ceiling bowl without even turning on the light, so that was no place for anything bigger than an idea. Finally I got out my wallet and poked it in among my own calling cards. It was hard enough finding a receipt I needed there, let alone a key to a fortune.

If it was a key; and even if it was, it was no good without the lock it opened.

The portfolio and travel brochures went separately into the wastebasket under a jumble of crumpled typewriter sheets, Kleenexes, cremation coupons, and a week's worth of ashtray exhaust.

Then because I couldn't put it off any longer I called Palm Volker to tell her about Càndido. She answered out of breath. I asked if she was okay.

"I'm up to my eyes in debt; otherwise peachy-keen. I was running a heat lamp over the Snipe. Going to take it up for a shakedown soon as the dope's dry. Are *you* okay? You sound like your rich aunt died and left it all to her dermatologist."

"Close." I brought her up to date, leaving out what I'd found on the back of the business card. I didn't know how to fit that into the conversion, or for that matter into the work at hand.

After a few minutes of silent listening her respiration had slowed to deadly normal.

"I knew about his past," she said. "He told me himself when he came here. Working with some of the types I've known in some of the places I've been, you get over being choosy. Between us, I've reached the point where I'd rather take a chance on someone who can't be trusted, because I can trust that. In all his time with me he never took a sick day or padded out a single time card."

"You can't judge character based on current behavior," I said. "Some things fester, then burst out just by overhearing an opportunity, like an old barnstormer sharing confidential information with his deaf wife at the top of his lungs."

"Where does that leave you?"

"Your guess is better than mine. I can't be trusted even not to be trusted. A couple of hours ago I had the whole case sewed up. The killers are working in tag teams this season. They've got me surrounded."

"Time for you to tag off, Amos. Leave it with the police."

"Not just yet. I've got a club. It may lead to spades. I need to draw from the deck."

She said, "Is that bridge? I thought we were talking about wrestling."

"I'm no good at either. I'm counting on beginner's luck."

Some kind of light aircraft lifted off within range of her telephone. It sounded like it was driven by a rubber band. She raised her voice. "Whenever something down here stumps me, I take to the air."

"That sounds like an invitation."

"It's whatever you want it to sound like. See you in a few."

The weather gods were having a high old time, like little boys burning ants with a magnifying lens. It was warm enough to switch off the heater, and before I got to the airfield, to shrug out of the light topcoat I'd put on in case the climate changed again. The windsock on the edge of the single runway twitched and shrugged, undecided, like a traveler at a crossroads. The sun had evaporated most of the puddles there. It seemed the sleet storm had cut a swath south of the neighborhood, grazing it only. Ocher dust billowed at the edge of the field, churned up by the ongoing parade of bulldozers and skid steers; if they were making any progress at all it was invisible to the naked eye.

A note was stuck to the door of the trailer office as if with a wad of Major Jack Flagg's gum. I recognized Palm's deceptively left-handed slant:

> Amos—
> Help yourself to a drink. I'll be back to pick
> you up.
> P.

She'd drawn a pair of loops onto the initial, like a set of wings.

I went inside. The bottle of Ten High stood on the desk beside a pair of pony glasses, the level a little lower than we'd left it after our tea party. I dribbled a couple of inches over two lumps of ice from a steel bowl and took a tour. The propeller still hung cockeyed on the wall; it threw the room off-kilter, as if the trailer had slid off one of its blocks. There were photos in pasteboard frames of various models of aircraft, like a proud owner's racehorses now out to stud: boat-shaped seaplanes, tubby troop carriers, Alaskan bush rangers custom-designed for setting down on the sides of mountains; their uneven landing gear made them resemble vaudeville drunks. More than a couple looked like death traps, flying crazy quilts patched all over like Clem Kadiddlehopper's overalls.

Palm and a very tall rooster with an eleven o'clock shadow and a lot of wavy black hair stood in front of a single-engine affair in some scrubby desert, dressed identically in open-necked shirts, riding breeches, and stovepipe boots. I guessed the beanpole was her ex-husband; he looked easy to hate. A smaller Palm, aged about fourteen and built like a boy, held an engraved plaque in both hands under a banner reading BOONE COUNTY FAIR. I couldn't read the words stamped on the brass plate, but it had an image engraved on it. She'd said she was a military brat; that covered a lot of geography. She'd put on more since, from Nome to Guadalajara. Palm again, all grown up in a tank top, braless, face streaked with grease, knelt grinning over a tangle of rusty handlebars and twisted tailpipes that might someday assume the shape of a road-ready Indian. I had to grin back. She looked like she was unwrapping Christmas.

I passed on to the picture I'd seen before, of a fragile-looking double-decked craft pawing the ground, eager to join battle with the bloody Boche. I'd seen its twin, or maybe the very same ship, in the Golden Eagle hangar that morning. It hadn't looked anywhere near in shape to fly, but then anyone who could build a motorcycle out of a pile of scrap metal could turn a bathmat into a flying carpet. I'd been busy myself in the hours since.

The bargain-brand whiskey tasted great, like I'd just got out of stir. I returned the glass to the desk—returned it with regret—and went outside, crunching ice between my teeth. I knew where I'd find her. All roads led to Golden Eagle ever since Clare Strick-ling's had ended there.

The bike leaned on its kickstand next to the hangar. It was a brief walk from the office, but she'd be too eager to get back to her new-old baby to take the time. In front of the open door, the Snipe rested on its tail skid and nose wheels, set squarely in a shaft of sunlight as if someone had worked out the composition before-hand. There in the open, freed of any restraint apart from the wheel chocks, it looked bigger than it had inside the hangar, and better than its picture. Its double-decked wingspread was wider than the homicidal Piper's; it looked too wide for the building to have contained it. The wheels, flat enamel like the ones that come with toy cars, and solid-rubber tires tilted the nose upward, ready to lunge toward the sky. Its new skin was spotless khaki. The bottlecap-shaped nacelle up front gleamed mirror bright, its wooden propeller varnished high yellow. The wing struts canted forward, thrusting the upper wing in front of the lower. Every-thing in the engineering suggested constant advance, no room for retreat.

"I know what you're thinking: She looks naked without her Lewis guns. I've been surfing the Net for every redneck gun show in the country; looking for dummies, of course, with their barrels plugged. Although it would be sweet to kick some dust out of the ground with a dozen rounds or so, give the rubes a thrill, as Major Jack says. These days it takes more to raise a gasp from an audi-ence than it used to."

Palm had stepped down from a mounting block near the nose of the plane, carrying a red metal gas can. She had on her jodhpurs and calf-high boots, with some extra items borrowed from Ame-lia Earhart's slop chest. A sheepskin leather jacket encased her to her hips and she'd knotted a white silk scarf loosely around her tan throat. Her wind-freshened cheeks glowed. A slight scent of gasoline wafted my way; coming from her it might as well have been *Soie de Paris*.

I hadn't been thinking about Lewis guns at all, but I went along. "It looks lethal enough as it is." I pointed at a feature that was fresh since that morning: a stern stylized face wearing a coonskin cap.

"Squadron commanders weren't as tightass then as now. They let the airmen express themselves. They were all boys, remember; twenty was almost retirement age. I don't know what the original pilots chose, so I came up with a design of my own." She narrowed her eyes, looking at me. "You don't like it?"

I moved a shoulder. "I don't know much about art. I only know what I like."

I even managed to put on a grin.

TWENTY-NINE

"Care for a spin?" she said.

I was expecting that.

"Is it legal?"

"Who knows? FAA says one thing, Civil Aeronautics another. The historic vehicle permits that apply to classic and antique automobiles don't work for planes. No ID number's required as it is for most civilian craft; then again maybe it is. On the other hand, how will the sky cops identify us without one?"

"Sure. A hundred-year-old fighter plane in metropolitan Detroit? Be like looking for a haystack on a needle."

"Do what everyone else does: Blame the bureaucracy. The older the machine, the longer you wait for the paperwork. Meanwhile we can buzz the city. They can't pull you over in the sky. I'll take care of any flak that comes later. You're just the innocent passenger. Be a sport."

"Is it safe? I should've asked that first."

"If Jack wasn't pulling my leg about the amount of hours on the engine since its last overhaul, we're ducky."

"He do that often? Pull your leg about, say, the likelihood of a fatal crash?"

She went on as if I hadn't spoken. "Even if it craps out, we can glide. If it busts a wheel strut, it wouldn't be the first time for this crate, and here it is. In the old days the pilot climbed out onto the wing and wrapped it in surgical gauze, and the ship would run steady meanwhile, if it didn't run into a thermal or a flock of geese, or if the mixture in the tank wasn't too rich. I wasn't kidding when I said these things have been known to land themselves with a corpse at the controls."

"How nice for the corpse."

"Any landing you walk away from is a good one."

"What about parachutes?"

"We won't be flying high enough for one to deploy in time to avoid making a mess when you touch down." She beamed ear to ear. "Whasamatter, you chicken?"

"I wish. Chickens can fly."

The Snipe had two cockpits—scoop-shaped openings—one in front of the other, to accommodate the pilot and the observer. I walked up to the one in the rear, the one I'd be riding in, grasped the frame with both hands, and gave it a shake. It swayed and rattled like a baby carriage and the whole plane shuddered.

I turned to face her. "What the hell. People who die in bed don't get their obituaries pasted in scrapbooks."

"That's my big brave P.I." She kicked the mounting block back level with the rear cockpit, hoisted herself up on one foot, reached inside, and alighted with a silver-colored helmet in her hand and another under her arm. She handed one to me. It was made of fiberglass or some other lightweight but durable material and lined with foam rubber under black vinyl, with a black-tinted plastic face shield, built-in headphones, and a Madonna-type microphone curving around in front.

"They're not as romantic as the old leather bonnet," she said, "but they're a big improvement. I borrowed them from the Major; rented, actually. Don't mix up his letting me play with his plane before I decide to buy it with any tendency toward generosity. If either of us backs out of the deal, the old scoundrel will have had it fixed up for free. Ever ride in a helicopter?"

"Before you were born."

"Bet you did. In case you forgot: Push this button when you want to talk, otherwise I wouldn't hear you if you were sitting in my lap."

I put it on and yanked the strap tight under my chin. Light as it was it made me feel top-heavy; I must have looked like I had water on the brain. The face shield tipped down just past the bridge of my nose. It was UV protected: Everything looked as sharp as if it were cut with a laser. I said something along those lines.

She was pushing fistfuls of chestnut hair under the edge of her own helmet. "The old-fashioned goggles had glass lenses. The pilots had to shuck them in a hurry if it looked like they were going to crash. They could shatter and leave you blind."

"Wouldn't want that. I'd like to see the ground coming up at me in glorious Technicolor."

"There's a coat in your cockpit. Bundle up. No central heating in the sky."

I could reach inside without using the block. I scooped up a red-and-black-checked mackinaw, stuck an arm in one sleeve, and stared. This cockpit, designed originally for the observer—a second pair of eyes to look out for enemy aircraft and man the rear-mounted machine gun while the pilot concentrated on maneuvering the ship—contained a stick for raising and lowering the nose and a cradle-like mechanism for steering the plane with your feet. The features crowded a space that was already cramped.

She saw my reaction. "It was converted into a trainer after the Armistice, with dual controls in front and in back. They're fully functional; the Major wouldn't get rid of them. If something went wrong with the set in front, all he had to do was climb out and crawl into the back; in midair, traveling at freeway speeds. Once a daredevil, always a daredevil. Don't touch them, whatever you do."

She spun around, kicked the block forward, then turned back. "Oh, there's no seat belt. If it gets bumpy, just hang on."

Before I could respond to that she swung herself over the side and into the pilot's seat like a cowgirl mounting up.

I didn't try to imitate her; my joints had a hundred thousand more hours on them and it was a tight fit. Those old knights of the air must have been recruited from the jockey pool in Tijuana.

But I felt comfortably snug, like a cork in the neck of a bottle. The leather upholstery molded itself to my back and hips, providing lumbar support and at least the illusion of security. I tucked my feet under the steering cradle and prayed a charley horse or something wouldn't come along to make me jerk a leg and send us into a spin.

"Can you read me?"

I jumped at the voice in my ears; started to answer, then remembered to push the red button on the mike. "Doesn't someone have to start the prop manually, from outside? 'Contact, ignition,' and all that Errol Flynn stuff?"

"That's one concession the Major made, on account of his arthritis and Edna's deafness: had an electric starter installed. Welcome to Volker Airlines. We really move our tails for you."

The last was almost drowned out by the sputter and roar of the 150-horsepower motor thundering to life. The prop turned, spun, became invisible. The ship trembled its whole length, like an animal stirring from hibernation. Purely out of reflex I clutched the frame on both sides. The uneven eruption from the pistons smoothed out, the fabric stretched—again, like something belonging to a living creature—and we began to roll, bumping over the cracks and craters in the asphalt, the gravelly patches where it had been reclaimed by nature or gouged by the heavy equipment grunting and snorting like truffle pigs all over the field, as

it would have over the ruts, chuckholes, and furrows in the aero-
dromes of 1918.

Something creaked; the cables that ran from the front cockpit
to the tail, twisting the rudder. It sounded like someone stroking
a rubber balloon. We made a wide, wide turn, steering the nose
toward the windsock, which had come to life too, fluttering in the
opposite direction; we were heading into the wind.

We stopped. The engine changed pitch again, bawling now,
deafening—too loud even for the audio equipment built into our
helmets to overcome. It seemed to be roaring exclusively between
my ears. We started moving again. The wind rose, the slipstream
buffeting my face below the edge of the shield; there was no
windscreen front or aft. Palm had swept the long end of her scarf
over her shoulder, where it straightened out, fluttering like the
guidon of a company of charging cavalry. Our speed increased.
The hangars, trailer-office, and all the scenery between smeared
into a multicolored blur, then a white swipe. Faster. My stomach
lifted before the plane. And then the earth dropped away and we
were heading into a bank of dense cloud that hadn't looked nearly
so angry from the ground, as if we'd broken a rule of some kind
and there was no going back to beg forgiveness.

THIRTY

We flattened out at around a thousand feet—pure guess-work, as there was no altimeter or for that matter even a gas gauge; those old-time pilots kept track of the consumption by means of an internal clock. Greater Detroit spread out below us like a counterpane, relentlessly horizontal except for the brief rumple of skyscrapers downtown. The swimming pools of Grosse Pointe, Birmingham, and Bloomfield Hills made bright turquoise statements in implausibly green backyards. Cars and trucks crawled along the tangled freeways and the brutal black diagonal slash of Woodward Avenue, and beyond the borders tilled fields and clipped golf courses lay in perfect squares like mosaic tiles, obscured from time to time by wisps of cloud.

The Bentley droned monotonously. I hadn't slept well, hadn't eaten all day; my eyelids felt like sash weights. But just as they started to droop, Palm would make some adjustment in the motion of the plane that threw a fresh gust of wind into my face like a dash of cold water, firing up the electrolytes. It was caffeine, crack, and a good stiff belt all in one.

Alert now, I heard the crackle of her headset before she spoke. "How you doing back there?"

I pushed the button. "Dandy. I can see my house from here." The acoustics were good; I could hear my voice as clearly as if I were eavesdropping on someone else. It wasn't nearly as deep as I liked to think.

"Everyone should ride in an open cockpit at least once. Closed cabins took all the glamour out of flying." There was a short silence, then another crackle. "You said on the phone you had a club and needed spades. What's the club?"

I made a decision. I dug out my wallet—I barely had room to bend my elbow—and fumbled for the card from Clare Strickling's portfolio. My fingers were cold and stiff. I thumped the surface of the plane to get her attention and held the card up in both hands. The wind wanted to snatch it out of my grip.

She turned her head to look at it; not long. The string of numbers written in hasty ink was brief—especially so, considering what it represented—and I figured she was a quick study.

I put away card and wallet. "Take your pick: Switzerland, the Caymans, little Andorra in the belly button of the Pyrenees. One of their banks has a sealed account to go with that number. That's what Càndido was after; what Parrish was after: a piece of it, anyway, in return for not fingering him for Strickling's murder. Càndido kept his appointment with Parrish at Golden Eagle and killed him. It spared him the trouble of explaining he hadn't even gotten the twenty thousand Strickling had brought along to pay for his flight."

We cruised along in relative silence. Below us to our right, one long wave swept across the sky-blue surface of Lake St. Clair like a straight razor.

"So that's the club," she said. "Any idea as to the spade?"

I stroked the button with my thumb; pressed it. "How long did you live in Kentucky?"

"Kentucky?" Crackle. "That was a hundred years ago. I was just a kid. My father was an instructor in the training school at Fort Knox for six months or so; temporary gig. Who told you I lived there?"

"The wall in your office. You were awarded a plaque in Boone County. I didn't make the connection until I saw what you'd painted on this plane. The plaque was engraved with the same image: a character wearing a coonskin cap, like Daniel Boone's. Boone was a sharpshooter. The county named for him would have a rifle competition. The first time I saw you, you said you were a real tomboy. Football, Soap Box Derby, shooting contests."

I let go of the button. I didn't know if I was supposed to say "Over." Anyway she didn't come back on. We droned on steadily. I pushed again. "That was a sweet shot, hitting a kneeling man from across the street. Not many experts could match it aiming downhill. Personally I think that's one more long-distance shot than this case needed."

The sky rolled like a barrel. I grabbed hold of the sides of the cockpit in both hands. My internal organs stayed behind and I was looking up at the ground. The bawling of the engine swelled inside my head, pushing my temples out from the center.

We righted then. I sucked in air as if I'd just come up from underwater. My fingers were cramped on the cockpit's bentwood frame and my body was cased in clammy sweat.

Crackle. "Sorry about that, Amos. I wasn't expecting to be accused of murder."

"Murderers seldom are." My voice sounded flat in my ears, and I realized I'd forgotten to press the button. I corrected that. "You didn't give Càndido a chance to count the money in my safe; that spared him disappointment. He was expecting a cut of a much bigger prize for killing Strickling: The proceeds from a big investment in the microchip industry, based on Emmett Yale's move to corner the market.

"You went way out on a limb when you mortgaged the airfield," I said. "A chunk like Strickling's would've bailed you out, set you up in business for life. But you realized too late that an open homicide on the property could scotch the annexation deal with City Airport, and when your hired hand took it on himself to silence Gabe Parrish with a bullet instead of shakedown money, that made things worse. So *adios* Càndido."

We banked hard left. I was thrown against the side of the cockpit, bashing my ribs and emptying my lungs. I hung on tight, gasping to refill them.

She'd seen Strickling's account number, committed it to memory. Annoyances such as signature cards, fingerprints, and retinal scanners could be addressed later, after I fell out of an airplane.

We straightened out again. "Still there, lover?" she spoke into my ear.

"Parts of me, anyway."

"Game cock." She threw us into a series of steep dips: right, left, right left, like a bronc trying to throw off its rider. I lost contact with the seat, my feet with the floorboards. The wind snatched hold of my arms, trying to tear me loose. How she managed to hang on I could only guess, probably with a firm grip on the stick. I was afraid to touch mine; an inch one way or the other might throw us so far out of control even she wouldn't be able to restore it. I hung on with one hand, jammed the other into the tight space behind my back, got hold of the butt of the .38, and worked it loose. I hadn't breath to get back on the horn. Instead I aimed between her helmet and the top wing, a little to the right, and fired into empty air. She flinched visibly.

Crackle. "Damn stupid bluff, Walker. Who's going to land this crate if you shoot me?"

I said nothing; sent another bullet, this time a little to her left. Her right shoulder dropped and we went into a flat spin, a stomach-churning spiral; we lost a couple of hundred feet while I hung on literally for dear life.

When we leveled out, I said, "It doesn't have to be a kill shot. A pilot with as many hours as you've put in should be able to fly with one arm."

"No one's that good a shot in the air."

"Sure. I might nick a major artery and bleed you to death. Then there's the network of nerves, muscle, and joints that make the difference between a working limb and a chunk of firewood. Or I could miss all that and put a slug in your head; you may even have time to say 'I told you so.'"

"You won't take that chance."

"It's more chance than you're giving me. How long have you known Càndido?"

"He came to me last year. I told you that."

"You also told me you flew a mail plane in Zacatecas. When was that?"

Nothing. I made sure my thumb wasn't still on the button, but she flew on in silence. I pushed it again. "Doesn't matter: Longer than just since last year. According to Inspector Alderdyce, Càndido applied for asylum here in return for rolling over on the Mexican Mafia in Zacatecas. How many other off-the-record chores has he performed since you brought him back with you?"

"That's more than just a stretch," she said then. "Zacatecas is a big state. I could've spent five years there and never come into contact with a fraction of the population, let alone one Mexican national. Been to Mexicantown lately? They're stacked ten deep with more coming in every day."

"I'm trying to satisfy my curiosity, not make a case for court. The way it plays, after he came to you with what he overheard Major Jack telling Edna, you told him to keep you posted, but he exceeded orders and tried to cut himself in on the twenty thousand; whether he was ambitious enough to hope for a slice of the bigger prize, we may never know. Anyway he got the bright idea to send that plane after Strickling, eliminating him as a threat in case he decided to turn state's evidence, and in such a way that it might be written up as just a tragic accident. The cops could hardly expect anyone who worked at the field to admit even to involuntary manslaughter. But things went sour when gawkers rushed in and he couldn't recover the cash without exposing himself; sourer still when it turned out Parrish witnessed the murder."

I let go of the button, once again to give her a chance to respond. She didn't take it. I went on.

"Who was Parrish expecting when he set up that meeting at the Golden Eagle office to discuss blackmail terms? Not me: He was surprised enough when I walked in the door. Not your hired hand either. You had the most to lose if your arrangement with City Airport fell through. Càndido got greedy and killed Strickling; he couldn't be trusted to discuss terms with Parrish. Squeezing you would provide Yale's glorified bodyguard with a nice little tax-free nest egg when he retired.

"So that was his second unexpected visitor in a few minutes. A distraction like that could slow his reflexes enough that a bandolero with a pistol already in his hand could get off a shot before Parrish picked up the gun on the desk in front of him."

A long stretch went by while the throbbing of the motor was the only sound. Then: "Imaginative. Can you prove it?"

"Not a syllable. I'm strictly an idea man. The cops will have pieces I don't, I've got pieces they don't. Maybe together we'll build something a prosecutor can take to court."

We flew steady. An oily tang stung my nostrils; exhaust from the engine. Below the edge of our shields our faces would look like a minstrel show.

"Not if they put it together the way you have," she said then. "Càndido was maintenance, strictly cleanup. He could make sure the surveillance cameras around the Golden Eagle hangar were down when they needed to be, or even get the jump on a chiseler behind a desk—he was a loyal employee, like I said, followed orders, especially with a bonus involved—but he didn't know a flap from an aileron. Anyone can shoot a shakedown artist when he's got the drop on him; he could be trusted to do that. It takes practical experience to direct a plane through an open door from inside a closed space with no one in the pilot's seat. That'd be like threading a needle with your eyes closed. You said it yourself, Mr. Detective. I'm the one with the hours."

I was still digesting that when she came back on. "Oh, and you slipped up somewhere else. Daniel Boone never wore a coonskin cap. But who am I to destroy the myth?"

I didn't have an answer for that one either. I was too busy hanging on while the world swung around the wrong way on its axis. This time her left shoulder dropped and we corkscrewed upward at breakneck speed for what seemed a thousand feet; not that three or four hundred one way or the other made any difference to the passenger in back. We straightened finally, almost perpendicular to the ground, described an arch at the top of a parabola, hung there an hour, both of us upside down. I felt myself slipping free of the upholstery. My hands cramped on the frame hard enough to burst the knuckles, and still I was slipping. The gun in my right hand got in the way of a firm purchase on that side, but I didn't want to let go of it; that would leave her the only one in charge of a deadly weapon. I tightened my grip on the left side. It felt as if my fingers would punch holes in the tough fabric. I passed my arm across my chest to park the revolver under my other arm. The barrel bumped the frame, jarring my finger on the trigger. The gun went off. The bullet passed through hollow fuselage all the way to the front cockpit. Palm Volker's back arched. Her helmeted head lolled over to one side and we went back into a corkscrew, this time straight down, with nothing to stop us but Mother Earth.

THIRTY-ONE

We shook and shuddered violently; the plane groaned and wailed like a victim twisting on the rack. No engineer on earth could have designed the plywood frame that would stand up to that kind of stress. The fear flashed through my mind that Palm had found her way out of her mess; that she'd either decided to take me along purely from spite or had forgotten I was aboard or flat out didn't care who came with her.

That's if she were even alive. Her head in its helmet flopped with every spin of the plane, as if she hadn't control of the muscles of her neck; but for all I could tell I hadn't either. I was being buffeted around like a seed in a gourd, barking my ribs against the frame until it seemed they were being ground to bonemeal.

It didn't much matter if anyone was in control. I let go of the .38, not noticing nor caring whether it fell overboard, useless piece of metal that it was. I took hold of the smooth rounded surface of the stick and pulled back on it with everything I had.

The wailing increased; and just for good measure something cracked. The rushing air came up under my face shield and stung my eyes; tears raced along both temples and lost themselves in the lining of my helmet. I couldn't tell if anything was going on in the earphones, if Palm was taunting me as her last act or pleading for forgiveness or the screaming of the wind was drowning her out. I raised my right foot from the decking and touched the right side of the steering cradle with a toe.

Something happened. If I were driving a car I'd have thought I hit a pothole hard enough to strike sparks off the chassis, jarring my teeth to the roots. The wind changed direction. We weren't flying level, but we weren't plunging either. I placed my left foot on the cradle on the left side and tickled it.

That put us back into a spin.

Panicking, I jammed down hard on the right side. I didn't know a flap from an aileron any more than Càndido, but something moved in one of the wings on that side and we swung around into a flat turn.

I was afraid to look down; wasn't sure which way down was. I had no idea how far we'd plummeted, and if there was time to do anything before we struck the ground. That was freedom, in a way. With nothing to lose I stroked the left side of the cradle with the ball of my foot. We reversed directions. I let up and so did the plane. We were still descending, but at an angle now instead of vertical.

It was an improvement; but like the fellow said as he was falling off a skyscraper, "So far so good." What was it Jack Flagg had said? *That model killed more Yanks than the Spanish flu. The minute it figures out you don't belong in the saddle, boy howdy! Run you straight into the ground.*

I risked a glance over the side. The patchwork quilt of the countryside was still a good distance below. It was enough to make you wonder if having a parachute might be worth the risk of it not opening in time to do you any good. I'd never pulled a ripcord, but it seemed simpler than landing a plane, and it was at least something to do.

There was a jerk. The plane went into a shallow bank. I yanked my feet off the cradle; but it wasn't anything I had done. I looked straight ahead. Palm was moving now, her shoulders working this way and that. She was back in charge. We came out of the bank and then we were flying parallel to the earth. Then we began to descend—gently.

Ten years, a hundred, twenty minutes; however long it was, the details of greater Detroit took shape, then the orderly spaced hangars and concourse of City Airport, followed by the haphazard arrangement of the buildings belonging to Palm's airfield. We made a lazy yawing turn, and I saw by the stirring of the windsock that we were heading into the wind: landing.

Not smoothly. Just as the ground came close enough to look as if I could bail out and jump, we struck down hard: Something crunched and we listed sharp left, hurling what was left of my rib cage against the frame as we slewed almost all the way around in the direction we'd come; bumped, bounced, and scraped earth with a grating noise, then coming to a stop that put a bruise on my chest I still feel when the barometer's low. The landing gear on the left side had collapsed.

She'd said that any landing you walk away from is a good one. It was for me, but not for her. When I found strength enough to hoist myself over the side, and footing enough to walk to the front of the plane, Palm Volker sat slumped over the front of her cockpit, one dead hand still gripping the stick.

THIRTY-TWO

etective Sergeant Gröstark adjusted his gold-rimmed glasses for a closer look at the propeller on the wall in Palm Volker's office. He took hold of it in both hands, lifted it clear, and leaned it in a corner. A 30–30 Remington rifle with scope attached hung on brackets at the same untidy angle. The propeller had hidden it completely.

"Smart," he said. "Hang the prop crooked: draw attention to it, so of course it must be harmless. Dumb: Seen it before. My three-year-old nephew knows all about reverse psychology. The best place to hide something is out of sight."

Alderdyce grinned at me; actually at the face I made. "Gröstark's our amateur shrink. We got another sergeant who's a cophouse lawyer, a lieutenant who's in real estate, and a third-grader who pulls coins out of his nose onstage in Harper Woods. I'm the only detective in the precinct."

I was sitting behind the desk; my legs had gotten me that far after I touched ground, but I was still waiting for my stomach to land. I wasn't airsick; I was just sick. "Dig a thirty-thirty out of Càndido?"

"Yep, only the name's Luis Garcia: That's John Smith in Spanish. Can't think why he bothered to change it. The State Department came through with his rap sheet when we convinced them he'd ratted out his last drug lord. He drove and maintained get-away cars for the Mexican cartel and did some killing on the side; they're Juans-of-all-trades down there. Our little Lady Lindy got her money's worth."

The morgue wagon had come and gone. A bullet in the liver doesn't give you much time to set a plane down gently, but she'd almost made it at that. I wouldn't be sleeping for a while. It had been a long time since a beautiful woman had cared enough about me to throw me out of an airplane.

"You've got the rest," I said. "Tomorrow okay to stick a fork in it?"

"Take all the time you need, as long as you're in my office at eight sharp." He held up my Chief's Special in a gallon Ziploc; he or one of his team had fished it off the cockpit floor. "Got to hang on to this for a spell. The chief likes to play cops-and-robbers with the real thing."

"Keep it as long as you like."

"I don't like. They come in all the time. Some days you can't open a door."

I said nothing. I hung a cigarette on my lip and got it going with both hands.

He wandered over to the wall and looked at teenage Palm holding her plaque at the Boone County Fair. "You can hardly see what's on the plate. How'd you know it was a coonskin cap?"

I staggered smoke at the ceiling. "Let me know if your precinct needs a psychic."

Most of the next morning was spent at the Second, drinking Lestoil Classic Roast and answering questions on four killings for the record. After that I had no place to go so I went to the office. I was getting so I could use stairs, if I leaned on the railing and didn't look down. I wasn't behind the desk five minutes when Emmett Yale called.

Twenty minutes later we were riding in a Yale town car behind a chauffeur in a Russian tunic with a garrison piece under his arm. The windows were tinted charcoal gray and the seats were covered with some kind of suede that had cost more than my Cutlass when it was new. I wanted to stroke it, just to see if it would arch its back against my hand. I wasn't anywhere near a hundred percent.

We were riding was all. Neither of us felt like sitting around an office; not even one as swank as his. The auto magnate's Roman-coin profile might have been cut with a fret saw against the smoky glass on his side.

"You're absolutely sure what happened to my stepson had nothing to do with Clare Strickling and what happened to him and Parrish."

I nodded. "Even if it was Lipton who leaked the stock deal to Strickling, which we'll never know. Strickling had already made arrangements to skedaddle; that's why the numbered account overseas. Flagg, the proprietor of Golden Eagle Excursions, says they'd settled on a fare weeks ago. There was no reason to button Lipton up if he was going to flee U.S. jurisdiction anyway. It was just another senseless shooting inside city walls. You wonder why the press even bothers to report them."

"What about the twenty thousand the police confiscated?"

"The SEC will have a hard time proving it was part of what he got from insider trading. If Strickling has any relatives, they'll have a claim, if there's anything left when the lawyers get through. In any case you won't see a penny of it, or of anything he made on the deal. Why should you? Your books balanced."

"You've earned a bonus."

"Not from where I sit. The job was to tie Strickling to Lloyd

Lipton. Instead it killed four people who had nothing to do with your wife's son. One of those killings was mine."

"That was an accident, you said. And she was trying to kill *you*."

"Maybe. Maybe not. I think she'd had enough. The sad part is she was too young to know what enough is. Too young all around." I touched the window button, but I didn't press it. You never know what effect fresh air will have.

I read a street sign. "Tell your man to turn this bus back downtown. I've got a living to make, hopefully with less dying."

You don't get rid of men like Yale that easily. He called once more, this time to offer me Gabe Parrish's old job in charge of security, with medical benefits, an expense account, and use of a company car; not the ocean liner he rode in, but not the model under federal investigation either. I said no thanks. It sounded like there would be flying involved.